HAYNER PLD/DOWNTOWN

W9-BXB-823

OCT 1 5 2009

# When the Buddha
# Met Bubba

# When the Buddha
# Met Bubba

Richard "Dixie" Hartwell

IROQUOIS PRESS

*When the Buddha Met Bubba*

Copyright © 2009 Richard "Dixie" Hartwell

All rights reserved.
This book or any part thereof may not be reproduced or transmitted in any form or by any means, electronic or mechanical, including photocopying, recording, or by any information storage and retrieval system, without permission in writing from the publisher.

Library of Congress Cataloging-in-Publication Data

Hartwell, Richard Dixie.
When the Buddha met Bubba / Richard "Dixie" Hartwell.
    p. cm.
ISBN 978-1-59652-527-6
1. Rednecks--Fiction. 2. Buddha--Fiction. 3. Alabama--Fiction.
4. Spiritual formation--Fiction. I. Title.
PS3608.A7877W47 2009
813'.6--dc22

                                        2009016304

Iroquois Press
An Imprint of Turner Publishing Company
200 4th Avenue North
Suite 950
Nashville, Tennessee 37219
(615) 255-2665
www.iroquoispress.com

Printed in China

09 10 11 12 13 14 15 16—10 9 8 7 6 5 4 3 2 1

F
HAR

b18860291

For Frances Lee and Tony Goggans with gratitude

# Chapter 1

I lost everything a man could lose. Just a few months ago, I had a real nice trailer over in Plantation Estates Mobile Home Park. But now the bank has it and everything else except my answering machine. I hid it from them just in case I ever got a phone again. You never know when you might get an important call. Sometimes when I get drunk I play old messages just to remind myself how it all came crashing down.

Beep! "Mr. Coker, this is Sand Mountain Electric. Your electricity will be turned off today unless a payment is made. Thank you."

Beep! "Billy Bob Coker, this is Southern Bell. You are three months behind on your payments and your telephone will be disconnected today unless we receive payment right away. Thank you and have a nice day."

Beep! "Mr. Billy . . . Coker, this is Scottsboro Water and Garbage, we haven't received a payment from you in two months. Your water will be shut off at the end of this business day. Thank You."

Beep! "Bubba, you can kiss my ass good-bye. You know I love you but I can't live with you anymore. I'm taking the cat and the pot-bellied pig. You can keep that beer-drinking, flea-bitten dog of yours. You two deserve each other. By the way, this is your former, soon-to-be ex second wife, in case you didn't know. I'm gonna live with my momma en'em over in Fort Payne until my Uncle Walker can get the papers filed for the divorce. Don't call me and don't come by. I swear to God if you do I'll have my cousin Wayne at the sheriff's office haul your ass to jail for wife abuse and it don't matter that there weren't none or not. I'll tell them there was and you know he'll believe me. I'll be praying for your sorry ass, 'cause if anyone needs it you do."

Us Southerners have a way of sticking it to one another but we always have to add "Thank you" or "Bless your heart" or "I'll be prayin' for ya." It's an unwritten code. After only three months of marriage, my second wife, Ginger, was so angry at me you'd think we'd spent a whole year or two together.

Hers was the last message I got. For two months I lived in my truck that—thank God—came with a camper shell when I bought it. I slept in it last November and December and nearly froze to death 'cause it didn't have a heater. The Sunshine Mortgage Company that held the note on it waited until the end of December before they came and repo'ed my truck.

With my ass in a sling, my life was turning into a genuine country song.

My second cousin on my mother's side, Skeeter Knight, is a big-shot manager over at Unclaimed Baggage. He offered me a job after my mother called his mother and she told him he had to help me 'cause we was kin. You may have heard of Unclaimed Baggage in Scottsboro, Alabama. It's the only thing Scottsboro has ever been famous for except for the Scottsboro Boys' trial of nine black men back in 1931, though we didn't call them "black" back then. Unclaimed Baggage has been on *60 Minutes* and *Good Morning America*. Doyle and Sue Owens opened it about thirty-six years ago. They started buying luggage that was left on buses and airplanes, sight unseen. They'd open them up and sell whatever was in them. People came from all over North Alabama and bought this stuff for a dime on the dollar. There were always colorful stories floating around about how people would buy a suitcase full of somebody's old clothes and find a diamond ring or a hundred-dollar bill.

Skeeter didn't want to give me the j-o-b. He's hated my guts ever since I peed in his gas tank for no other reason than he got a car before I did and I was the oldest and it wasn't right. It was just a Pacer but it still made me ill at him. Anyway, I was sitting in the Black Cat Bar and Grill downing a few cold ones and putting quarters in the jukebox. I listened to song after song telling me what a piece of shit I was for losing my woman, job, truck, and camper when Skeeter sees me going down for the third time in my beer. I tried to hide from him but he saw me anyways.

"Cuz, you don't look so good," he said with a grin as he pulled me by the hair off the bar. I reckon I went to sleep there for just a minute or two. "I saw yer mamma the other day in Food Land and she told me what's goin' on with ya. You really been living in your truck the last few months? Damn, that's bad. Guess you better come work for me at the store."

Skeeter's huge. He weighs about a thousand pounds and played guard for our high school football team. He still wears his high-school football letter jacket when a bunch of us get together to play cards even though it is about three hundred sizes too small for him. He wears his hair so short it's hard to tell if he's a fat ex-Marine or an escapee from a mental institution where they shave your head so they can attach electric shock wires up to you. You know how some people's personality fills up a room when they come in? Well, he didn't have a personality but he sure could fill up a room with his big mouth, boasting about his important position at Unclaimed Baggage. I mean he is the most famous person any of us know but he shouldn't keep rubbing it in.

"Here's my offer," Skeeter said. "You come work for me as a sorter and I'll give you $6 an hour and you can sleep in the back room until you get on yer feet. There'll be no drinkin' or druggin' or whorin' around back there. The Lord doesn't like it and I don't either. If I catch you doin' any of that, then that's it. Got it?"

"Uh-huh."

"You want the job, then come in first thing Monday morning. We'll find you some work clothes at the store. This whole black T-shirt," he said pulling it until it was stretched all out of shape, "and jeans and Dingo boots thing has got to go. And get you a haircut. You look like a damn hippie."

I could barely get in a word edgewise so I just said, "Thanks, Cuz, I'll take it. I don't have much choice. I won't give you any trouble. I've had all of that I can handle for a little while. One thing though. Could you give me a little walking around money? I'll pay you back when I get my first check."

"Sure Bubba, here's twenty. Don't drink it all up. See you Monday morning bright and early. And for God's sake go to church this Sunday and make your momma proud. Act like you got some raising."

So now thanks to my momma and Skeeter's momma I live in a small room in the back of Scottsboro's most famous tourist attraction. I work with Chigger Suggs, my best friend since elementary school. Chigger is a small guy, who kinda looks like the kid who played the banjo in one of my all-time favorite movies, *Deliverance*. You know, that's the movie with Burt Reynolds that scared city folk half to death. At least it kept them away from here, for fear we were all inbred freaks chasing after our sisters and first cousins. Chigger's daddy gave him his nickname because he was always pestering him and has this weird little head.

Baggage arrives by the ton-load from nearly every airline in the world and boy hidey let me tell ya' people try to take some weird ass shit on a plane. Last week we got a leaf blower, two DustBusters, three toilet plungers, and a car bumper from a '57 Chevy and a suit of armor, the kind knights wore. We also get the stuff security confiscates—fourteen cans of WD-40, a machete, and six mousetraps. It all comes here.

We sort through everything and make sure we find the good stuff and separate it from the crap. What we don't put on the floor, Skeeter's momma comes and gets and loads up in her golf cart because that's all she can drive since she got her license revoked for doing eighty-five in a fifteen-mile-an-hour school zone. Jimmy Ray, the cop that pulled her over, asked her where she was going in such a hurry. She told him the First Church of Nazarene was having a huge yard sale that morning and she wanted to be the first to get there. When he went to sit in his car to write her a ticket she tore off like a bat out of hell. He went after her but then gave her a few minutes to load the things she bought before taking her to the courthouse. Sometimes she has to make six or seven trips to Unclaimed Baggage just to haul it all back to the trailer park where she and Skeeter live. She sells it each August at the world's largest yard sale. Boy you should see it. It's like all the K-Marts and Wal-Marts, and Dollar General stores exploded at the same time and it all landed on a four-hundred-mile stretch from Florida to Ohio and people descend on it like a herd of deer on a salt lick. You can get thirty or forty pairs of socks for about two bucks.

Spring was coming on and I'd been working at Unclaimed Baggage for three months when I decided to go to Henagar to visit my first wife, Shirley. It was Saturday and I thought it was time to try and see her and my son who goes over there on the weekends to fix anything that's broke. I was pretty sure my boy's birthday was coming up, so I was going to give him a twenty-dollar bill. I'd finally saved just enough money to do that and buy me a very used pickup.

Robert Earl, my second cousin, drove me. Now you'd like my cousin, dumb as a sack of hammers, but he's a good ole boy. He's blind in one eye and can barely see out of the other one so when he's driving he hunkers down on the steering wheel with his bad eye shut and his good eye bulging out like he was taking aim at the road. In daylight, he scares passing drivers so much they have to pull off the road and wait for Cyclops to barrel through before they're composed enough to keep driving.

As soon as we arrived, Shirley flew through the front porch and into the front yard.

"Told you the last time you came up here drunk as Cooter Brown not to set foot on my property unless you were coming to apologize to me and Lucius. Now you get the hell out, ya hear? We don't want nothing to do with your sorry ass. Who's that?" She pointed to Robert Earl who was leaning against the truck and petting my dog, Blue, who had his head stuck out the window.

"That's just my cousin Robert Earl. He's carrying me over to Wheels for Steals so I can buy me a used truck. I wanted to come by and say hello and give Lucius some money for his birthday. I reckon it's coming up soon, ain't it?"

She sneered at us as she wiped her hands on the apron my mother made for her as a wedding present.

"Sorry about the last time I visited," I said. "I know I shouldn't oughta done it. I was drunk and had no business talking to you like I did. Will you accept my heartfelt apology?"

I was terrible-acting that day. My second wife had just left me,

I'd lost all my stuff, and I was having a real good pity party. Sometimes I get mean when I'm drunk on hard liquor and that was one of those times.

"All right then. I reckon you're forgiven." She threw up her hands and pursed her lips. "Lucius went to the store to get me my smokes. You'll have to ask his forgiveness when he gets back if you're still here."

"Mighty kind of you," I said.

She lit up a Marlboro. "I guess all you rednecks have to drive a truck? It's like the law or something. But what the hell do you need a truck for? You don't own anything."

"To haul stuff."

"What stuff?"

"The stuff I'd have to haul if I had a truck to haul it in."

She rolled her eyes. "Get the fuck outta here. You never did make a lick of sense."

With my first wife, Shirley Crowe, what you see is what I got. She was the prettiest girl in high school with a mouth like Chris Rock, and a body like Jessica Simpson. She's got eyes as green as an old coke bottle and hair that looks like Marilyn Monroe's. Her momma said she didn't have much of a brain under that hair or she'd never have married me. She didn't think much of my natural intelligence either.

On our wedding day Shirley told me her momma whispered in her ear as she was walking down the aisle, "I'm telling you, you shouldn't marry that boy. Like the country song says, 'When it comes to brains, he got the short end of the stick.'"

Shirley and I met in high school. I was one of those black sheep, outcast guys who didn't really fit in anywhere. I wasn't a jock or a geek. I guess you'd call me an outlaw—I smoked, drank, and screwed around. Shirley was raised in a strict Church of

Christ family that tried to discourage their members from having sex because it looked too much like dancing, which they are really against. They wouldn't even let their own church have a piano or nothing. They said Christians were supposed to "make a joyful noise" and boy could Shirley do just that in the back of my old Ford Econoline van.

On the other hand, my family was members of the Full Gospel Charismatic Second Antioch Church of the Pentecost, or Holy-Rollers for short. We had guitars, drums, tambourines, and an electric organ. About half of us got drunk on Saturday night and screwed and danced our asses off and almost never felt guilty because we knew we were going to get washed in the blood of Jesus on Sunday morning. Our reverend Hawk Hawkins always told us not to tell anyone that we spoke in tongues and handled snakes and drank strychnine ever once in a while, because he said he didn't want a bunch of weirdos come to church just to gawk at us.

My people are all from Sand Mountain where they still do that stuff. But I ain't set foot in a church since Shirley and I got married on graduation day. We missed our graduation ceremony because she was already showing. We got married that day 'cause her daddy was real fond of her and his shotgun but wasn't too keen on me. Six months later we had our son Lucius Gene and the very next day she asked for a die-vorce. She said she waited until then 'cause she didn't want to bring a bastard child into this world. That sort of thing still counted back then. I haven't been around much ever since.

Just as Robert Earl and I were about to leave and go truck huntin', my son came driving up. Lucius is twenty-one or twenty-two years old. He's a good-looking boy, if I do say so myself. He is tall and slender. His momma says he works out real regular. He has brown hair like his momma's, well I mean like hers before she dyed it a color not found in nature. He has a temper like my daddy's.

"What the hell you doing here old man? I thought Momma told you not to come around here." He started towards me with his fist doubled up.

"Now wait a minute, Son, I was just . . ."

"I don't give a good goddamn what you were just. And don't call me 'son.' You're just a sperm donor. You'd have to be a father to have the right to call me that and you gave up that right a long time ago. Get your beer-drinking, sorry ass in the truck and leave us be."

"Now listen here, you're not too big for me to whup. You don't talk to me like that; I'll kick your ass all over Henagar, goddamnit!"

Shirley shouted, "Bubba, you better git now!" She looked at Lucius. "Son, come on in here. We don't want the police called on us again."

After giving me a sideways glance, he said, "Did you apologize to her for the last time?"

"That's between me and your ma." I pulled the twenty out of my billfold and wadded it up and threw it at him. "Happy goddamn birthday, you ungrateful little bastard."

"I guess that's what a son is who doesn't have a father. Screw you, old man." He went inside and me and Robert Earl went to Fort Payne and drank the whole weekend away.

When I finally stumbled back to my room in Unclaimed Baggage early Sunday morning, I could see that somebody had moved stuff around. There were suitcases piled up everywhere. One of them was this old Samsonite we got in on Tuesday that looked to be a hundred years old. It was imitation snake skin and faded yellow. It had travel stickers all over it from Paris, Rome, New York, Istanbul, Greece, Korea, China, Japan, and Jerusalem. It was wrapped with duct tape and a Bungee Cord. I mean it, who travels with a piece of crap suitcase like that? I started to throw it in the garbage bin behind the store where we toss the shit that even Skeeter's momma can't sell. I don't know what compelled me, but I took the old, beat-up suitcase and put it in my room with about a hundred others.

Later that night I bought a bottle of Southern Comfort to ease off the hangover. I shrugged on one of Jesse Jackson's fancy suits. Last week, we got two suitcases full of them. Don't ask me why the airlines couldn't return these. He had his name on everything including his dang underwear so it wasn't that they didn't know who they belonged to. I grabbed a football helmet that was in a duffle bag. I walked over to my little frigerator to get Blue a beer, when the room started shaking all of a sudden like. The suitcase with all the stickers fell right on the top of my head. It would have knocked me out cold if I hadn't had on that helmet. All the lights went off and Blue and me was just standing there in the dark, latched on to each other, when this voice said, "Trust Me."

First thing I thought was it must be Chigger and one of his inbred friends just messin' with me.

"All right, Chigger, you asshole, come on out. I'm going to whup your ass, you pesky little son-of-a-bitch." I pointed my flashlight and pointed out into the store but there wasn't anybody there.

"TRUST ME!"—the voice screamed. I swear on my momma's head a bright light started seeping out of the suitcase. My first thought was that I'd stumbled upon a talking bomb. If them terrorists could make a shoe explode, then they could probably make a suitcase light up and talk.

My hands were shaking so hard that I could barely take off the Bungee Cords and unwrap the duct tape holding it together.

After I pulled off all the tape I heard bells ringing. The lamp on my bedroom table got really bright. I lifted the lid and green light damn near blinded me for about thirty or so seconds. I rubbed my eyeballs. Scared as I was I searched its contents.

Now what I saw didn't make any sense. All that was in that suitcase was a bunch of pictures. There was this one of a huge snake that coiled around itself; it was brown, white, yellow, and rust. In the center was a circle with other circles around it and the snake's head was touching the center circle.

Under it was another picture of a stained-glass window like the ones you see in rich people's churches. It was made up of these circles of roses with one rose in the middle and was red and green and white. Under it was a picture of a painting that looked like an Indian drawing of some kind and it was black and white and under that was a picture of something that looked real Oriental.

I looked at each one and the more I looked the more nervous I got. I was afraid that some demons might be lurking around. I hated demons all my life because I saw our pastor cast them out right in church many a time. The poor souls who were possessed would carry on, screaming and pitching fits—kinda like an angry drunk but with a better vocabulary.

I finally turned each picture over and saw there was writing on the back. The first said—A Dreaming from Australian Aborigine. On the second—Rose Window in Grace Cathedral. The third one said Navajo Sand Painting, and the last one said, A Buddhist Mandala. Below that one was written: Whoever finds these paintings is ready to take a journey. It was signed "Pu Tai."

# Chapter 2

I was dizzy and light-headed. The bells or chimes or whatever had stopped. My table lamp flickered, and then stayed on while the light inside the suitcase went out. Blue—who was hiding under my cot—whined softly as the room shook. I looked at the crate that served as my nightstand and saw a shot glass filled with whiskey ripple like in that dinosaur movie. Somehow I knew Blue and I weren't the only ones in the room.

I was terrified one second, then relaxed and drowsy the next. I dropped into bed and fell into the deepest sleep I've ever had.

When I woke up the next morning, my first thought was that I'd had one hell of a dream. I even considered tapering off the hard stuff and just drinking Blue's beer.

As I washed my face in the sink, I saw a familiar suitcase reflected in my bathroom mirror. I swallowed hard and blinked, but it was still there. My heart thumped in my chest and I was scared, but I ran back into my room and looked inside. There weren't any lights or sounds, but the weird pictures were still there. With a shudder, I closed the suitcase back up and wrapped it tight with some Alabama chrome (that's what we call duct tape in the south 'cause so many of our cars are held together with it).

When I finished with the tape, I tied the Bungee cords

around the suitcase and slid the whole mess under my bed.

All the stress I'd been under must have made me hallucinate. I needed a little R & R from my J-O-B so I could get my nerves calmed down.

Anxiety runs in my family. My momma was always worrying and fidgeting and my dad drank like a back-sliding Baptist preacher. I was getting to be like both of them. As a matter of fact that's how I came to have my beer-drinking bluetick hound. Blue was my daddy's dog, but he couldn't keep both of them in beer so he brought him over to my house about two years ago. That was the last I saw him until we were at Morris's Funeral Home for the viewing. That night he'd shaken hands too many times with his best friend, Jack Daniels, and ran into a big rock that wouldn't move to one side like me and my mother always had to when he'd had too much to drink.

I called Chigger and asked him if he wanted to hang out that night. He said he'd pick us a couple of bottles of wine. Wine never hurt anybody; they drank wine all the time in the Bible.

We decided to go frog giggin' 'cause two men can't go outdoors without killin' something or people might get the wrong idea. Besides, huntin' season hadn't started yet and frog giggin' always took the edge off. I had made my own gig by attaching a gardening fork to the end of a broomstick.

The only light I wanted to see for a while was the one I'd be shining in some old frog's eyes right before I sent his soul to his maker and his legs to a fryin' pan. A frog's hind legs can contain as much meat as the legs of a medium-sized chicken. Most people have never had frog legs really fried up just right. When they are they taste just like chicken. We gave up hunting frogs fifteen minutes after we started. I've always had a problem with sticking with anything for long.

At Bullard's pond we sipped Boone's Farm strawberry wine, which comes in a fancy bottle even though it only costs $3.50 and has a twist-off cap.

The cattails at the shallow end of the pond waved in the dark like skinny men bein' blown by the wind. The smell of cow pies filled the air, which wasn't an altogether bad odor once you're used to it. Chigger had the Allman Brothers Band cranked up on his car stereo. The night was cold and kind of damp and humid the way the last winter days can be in the South. We sat and sipped and listened to dead Duane's thunderous "Whipping Post." Ole' Chigger banged on his legs like they were Butch Trucks' drums. His dance consisted of him jumping up and down, flailing his bony arms in all directions. It looked like he was having a conniption. No wonder Baptists were against dancing.

He had brought four bottles of wine and by the third one I was telling him about the suitcase.

"You're shitting me, man. Why you wanna mess with my mind like that?" Chigger spit tobacco into the pond and wiped his mouth about half way.

"I'm telling you the god's honest truth. This voice just kept saying 'Trust Me.'" I thought back on the green glowing light and the weird-ass pictures and shuddered. "It was some freaky shit, I'm tellin' ya."

Chigger opened another bottle and smelled the metal top before throwing it into the pond. "So what are you going to do?"

"Nothing. What the hell you think I'm going to do? I was born at night but not last night. Hell, I may have dreamt the whole thing but when I woke up this morning there that suitcase was with those confusing pictures staring at me."

"Let me make a Chigger Sug-gestion. Find that fucker and give him his sorry-ass Samsonite. If he gives you ten dollars or whatever, what have you lost but a little time? And that's something you got plenty of, Bubba."

I used to hate it every time Chigger or anyone but my mother called me Bubba, which is what my daddy started calling me when he wasn't calling me some of his other favorite pet names like "retarded," "panty-waist," and "momma's boy." It makes me want to whup somebody's ass, mostly my daddy's. I mean for god's sake who starts calling their kid a name like Bubba before they're two years old? But after all these years I've gotten used to it I reckon.

"Well, like my granddaddy always told me," I said to Chigger, "I never had a pot to piss in or a window to throw it out of so when you got nothing, you got nothing to lose."

"I say go for it, goddamnit!"

"Chigger Suggs, if you give me another sug-gestion I'm going to puke."

The next morning I woke up, looked around my room, and took stock. A. I live in the back room of the Unclaimed Baggage making minimum wage. B. My best friend's name is Chigger. C. My other best friend is Blue, who is a bigger sot than I am. D. I got two ex-wives who would have me shot if they only knew someone from Mississippi. There are good ol' boys in the Bayou State that will come over to Alabama and kill someone for you for a case of beer and a hundred-dollar bill. They are so backwoodsy over there. At least that's what my granddaddy used to say.

I wasn't exactly climbing the ladder to success, more like I was fallin' off it. Hell, Chigger would get a promotion before I did 'cause he had seniority.

Part of me has always wanted to leave the South and see what other folks live like. Between Daddy's alcoholic craziness and my mom's teetotaling, there were whippin's, worshipin', hollerin', and holy-rollin'. I felt like a cross between Job and Jonah. The South is beautiful but it can swallow your whole life and if it doesn't spit you out you can get stuck forever, and end up in a white-trash trailer park, workin' in a junkyard or duckin' the law for makin' meth. Half my friends and cousins were cookin' crank and the other half was doin' time for it.

I've always wanted to know if there was something in me my daddy didn't see, that even I didn't see. Maybe Shirley saw something in me once upon a time. I remember one night before it got real bad she said, "Bubba, when I first met you, you were as shiny as a new copper penny. Now you're just plain rusty. Momma stayed with my father for thirty years hoping her love and devotion would allow her see that shininess in him again. But she never did. I won't stay with no man trying to polish him up for no thirty years." If I recall she was crying a little when she said it.

All day, I pondered my future and finally came to a decision. All I had to do was return the suitcase and maybe get some money this crazy guy might give me for returning it and these pictures.

So I ruminated and cogitated all night about how I was gonna find this guy. I finally went to sleep about two in the morning. Not long after, I woke up to the voice, "Trust Me. I'm right here. I don't have time to waste, so if Bubba won't come to the mountain, the mountain must come to Bubba." I had absolutely no idea what the hell that meant.

The suitcase started to quake and then the Bungee cords popped off and the duct tape split. The Samsonite opened and this big son-of-a-bitch came crawlin' out of it like a rabbit out of a hat. He was wearing a fancy Nancy pair of black pajamas and funny little black shoes. I screamed like a little girl.

"I'm not here to hurt you."

"You ain't real! I'm dreaming you. I've lost my mind. I'm going to wake up now. This is just a dream. Why can't I have one of a *Sports Illustrated* model or something? This isn't happening. I'm going to wake up and everything is going to be all right."

I closed my eyes for a minute or two and when I opened them there he stood. Now let me set the record straight right now. I'm no pantywaist. I've jumped off the cliffs at Whippoorwill Hollow into the Tennessee River and I've ridden on top of cars going real fast while playing chicken and many a time I've uttered the words, "Hey, I bet you never seen anybody do this before." But when it came to a half-naked Oriental popping out of a suitcase, I peed my pants.

# Chapter 3

"What'cha say, Bubba? How's it hanging?" The big guy said in an accent and a low, quietlike tone of voice. "I hope that is the way your people say it? I didn't have time to learn much Southern Appalachian before the Wise Ones sent me."

"How's it hanging? Here's a better question: Who the fuck are you? What are you doing here? You know what, it don't matter. Just crawl back in that suitcase and go back to wherever you came from!"

The guy stayed calm. "Allow me to explain. I have been sent by TWOS."

"I don't care who sent you! I don't care who you are or where you come from or where you're going so long as it's a ways from here.

He seemed confused, but didn't say anything. He must have weighed in at about 250 to 300 pounds. He had a short, coal-black ponytail. Actually he sort of looked like Steven Seagal, but not like he looked in *Under Siege* but his later movie when he got real fat.

"I'm going to lie down on this bed and I'm going to close my eyes and when I open them you'll be gone. Then I'll go to work and everything will be just like before. Okay, now I'm lying down. I'm closing my eyes, I'm asleep."

With my eyes still closed, I heard a big sigh.

"Rise up, Bubba. We have work to do. TWOS are serious about this. Trust me."

"TWOS what?"

"The Wise Ones. I was told your people like acronyms."

"Uh-huh."

"Trust me."

"Would you stop saying that? There ain't no way I'm trusting you." I cupped my hands over my ears like a damn four-year-old.

"Ahyyyyaaaayyyyyyyayyyyya. I can't hear you. You're not here. You're not real. I'm just having a fuckin' nervous breakdown. Bryce State Mental Hospital: get a rubber room ready for me. Tuscaloosa, here I come!"

All of a sudden I felt my cheek sting as his big hand connected with it.

"Come! I'm here. Respond to this moment. We have much work to do. Trust me."

I rubbed my face. "You ever slap me again, I'll open up a can of whup ass on your head."

He sat on the floor and burst out laughing for no apparent reason. He looked like one of them Laughing Buddha statues I seen in Chinese restaurants in Fort Payne.

"What is so goddamn funny? I don't see anything funny about this. Do you see something funny that I don't see?"

"I was just thinking one eternal moment I'm up there," he pointed to the ceiling. "I was wrestling Jacob—good man, pretty good wrestler—when I received the call to come to earth. Remember how your grandfather Coker and you loved to watch wrestling on television on Saturday evenings?"

"All I want to know is what do you want with me?"

"Later. First," he said, wiggling his fingers in the air, all girly-like. "Give me a tour of this interesting place of business."

I switched on the lights hoping no one would see us, not that there was much chance of that. The store is the size of two football fields full of racks of clothes with enough sporting goods to outfit all the teams of any sport played in Alabama. The blue-white neon lights lit up all at once. I knew if anybody saw me talking they really would think I was a passenger on the short bus. My overactive imagination was in complete control.

"What is this place?"

"Unclaimed Baggage. I work here. Wouldn't you know this if you really came from up there?" I pointed to the ceiling. Pu Tai smiled and shrugged his shoulders.

"Some things I know. Some I don't," he said as we walked through the store. He started touching everything and asking lots of questions.

"Nice guitar," I said as he picked up an old Martin as we were passing through the musical instrument section. He strummed a few chords from my favorite country singer—from Randy Travis' song "Forever and Forever, Amen."

"How do you know that? Are you from . . . heaven?"

"Some call it that. I prefer to call it Nirvana. But really that's just a name."

"I thought Nirvana was a band. My first cousin Gerald on my daddy's side is into that weird music and was playing it one day when I went over to take his momma some tomatoes from my momma's garden."

"No. Nirvana isn't exactly a place. It's more like a state of mind that you dwell in until TWOS send you back down to be somebody else or do something else that needs to be done."

That didn't sound very Christian-like and it made no sense, but we kept walking. It took forever to walk because he kept stopping in different departments and asking questions about everything. Finally, I just stopped him in the women's section and said, "Don't you folks up there in Nirvana have any of these things? Heaven has got everything or so I've been told."

"No. You see I haven't been down here in a long time so you are going to have to teach me a lot."

"Teach you, my ass. You've got to get out of here. I don't know you, and besides you're just a figment of my imagination anyway. I don't even know why I'm talking to you. Teach you? Bullshit."

"According to TWOS I'm supposed to teach and learn. Their exact words were, 'What we've been doing up here isn't working and what you people are doing down here isn't working either. It is time to put what we know up here with what they know down there.'"

"Thanks a lot, that really clears things up."

"So where am I going to sleep? You must be knowledgeable about sleep since you've been doing it all your life. No offense. I'm just very tired. I had to travel a great distance and I need a rest."

"How the hell do I know where you are going to sleep? You can't stay here. My room is barely big enough for me. You've got to get back in your suitcase and go back and tell TWOS I sent your ass packin'. Like I've said all along, I'm going to wake up in the morning and all of this is going to be forgotten."

He looked sad.

"But since you're not real anyway, I guess it won't hurt none for you to sleep on the floor with Blue. Looks like he's slept through all of this. I gave him way too much beer before he went to bed. Blue ain't no watchdog, that's for sure, but he's a good ol' boy."

I threw a couple more blankets on the floor and made a pallet for the big guy. He fell asleep as soon as he hit the floor. I went to bed and just before I dozed off I thought to myself, so this is what it is like to lose your mind.

# Chapter 4

I woke up the next morning and nearly jumped out of my skin 'cause he was still there, this guy lying on my floor like a big boy dog. I still wanted to believe I'd dreamed this whole shit up, but there was Blue with his muzzle wedged in the guy's armpit, and both of them were snoring. I kept rubbing my eyes and cursing to myself for having the crazy gene that had been passed down through my father's family tree, which only had the one or two branches on the count of everybody kept marrying their cousins back in the old days to keep what little land they had in the family.

I got up, got dressed, and started shaking him and my dog. Blue kept sleeping but the fat fella finally woke up. "You want some coffee, big guy?" His coal-black hair was all over his huge head.

"Thank you, but I only drink tea. Do you have some green tea? You know it's much better for you than coffee. It has all these antioxidants, helps prevent cancer, and helps with weight loss."

"It doesn't look like it's helped you."

"You should have seen me before I started drinking tea—see I've taught you something already. What are you going to teach me today?"

"Not a goddamn thing. I need you to get outta here before Skeeter comes in and finds you."

"I'm not going anywhere."

"Why?"

"Because I am already here."

"But I want you to be somewhere else."

"You can't get somewhere else until you accept where you are."

I started rubbing my temples. "I'm getting a headache."

"I'm glad we cleared that up. We must take a little trip. Until we leave together, I must stay here and meditate and prepare for the journey. We have only seven days to complete and achieve our goal. Would you be so kind as to bring me some tea?"

"First of all this is Unclaimed Baggage not a grocery store and second of all what do you mean we are going on a trip? I ain't got no vacation days coming for a long time. I got to work for a living."

"I wish you would just calm down and pay attention to me for a minute."

"Listen, you weird motherfucker, you can wish in one hand and shit in the other and see which one fills up first."

He seemed to think about that one for a while, then smiled as if he finally understood what I'd said.

"I'm going to work, but first I gotta take Blue out for a pee."

Blue and I walked out and I watched as he did his business. When we got back, this guy hadn't moved a muscle.

For the next eight hours I worked. I took two short breaks and a half-hour lunch. Each time I'd go back to my room and each time I'd find him sitting there staring a hole in the wall; his forefinger and thumb touching.

There I was in the cafeteria, staring at my bologna sandwich like it was a crystal ball. I was in the middle of thinking when Chigger pulled up a chair next to me. He nearly scared me to death 'cause I was deep in my head, which my granddaddy used to say, "Is a scary neighborhood and you wouldn't want to be caught in it after dark." No matter how deep I went I couldn't figure out how to get rid of my unwanted company.

"Hey, man, what the hell?" Chigger said. "Earth callin' Bubba, come in Bubba!"

"Huh?"

"You looked like you were on another planet."

"I wish I were, 'cause this planet is a little too weird today."

"What's up, man? Tell old Chigger your problems 'cause you ain't going to get on Doctor Phil. I am the man with the plan, Stan. You got the strain and I got the brain. Lay it on me."

Chigger is full of shit, but he means well. "This one I'm gonna' to have to figure out for myself. I'll talk to you after work."

When I got back to my room, Blue had his head on the guy's lap and was snoring again. How a guy that big could stay still and not fall over is beyond me.

"Hey you, you there contemplating your navel." I snapped my fingers and he slowly looked up at me. "I told you to be outta here when I got back from work. It's a good thing Chigger or Skeeter didn't come in here looking for something. If you are not going to leave I'll have to call the sheriff."

The big guy rose slowly and surveyed the room. "This is not where you are to end up. You have important work to do. Only then will I report to TWOS. So, in redneck speak, pack your shit and let's go!"

"Let me get this straight. I'm supposed to go gallivanting around somewhere with a strange, pajama-wearing, ponytailed guy who jumped out of a suitcase—"

"These are not pajamas."

"—Give up my job and walk out of here just like that. Is that what you are saying?"

"Ah, finally you understand. Took awhile, though. Blue got it on the first round."

24

Blue woofed and I felt my neck getting hot. "Well, that ain't fair. He's purebred."

"Let's get a move on, Pilgrim."

"Pilgrim, my ass, who do you think you are, John fucking Wayne?"

"The Duke is quite popular up there, but we have to keep him away from the horses. He hates them."

"Man. You do have a lot to learn. And I ain't goin' nowhere with you . . . you . . . I don't even know what to call you!"

"Pu Tai."

"Oh, yeah, I remember now. That's the name on one of those pictures in the suitcase. What's with those pictures anyway?"

"You'll see. Trust me."

"Pu Tai is a really weird name for down here. How 'bout I call you Pooh for short?"

"That is my name."

"No, P-O-O-H. You know, like Winnie the Pooh?"

"What is a Winnie the Pooh?"

"He was a bear in a children's story—trust me, the name fits. Now let's just pretend for a minute that you are real and that you came from up there and that I'm dumb enough to quit this dollar-a-week job and go waltzing off with you to God knows where. I suppose you wanna go to the Himalayas, right?"

"Wrong."

"China. Right?"

"Wrong."

"Tie-bet? That's gotta be it."

"Wrong again."

"Then where?"

Pooh paused for four or five minutes. He closed his eyes and held his thumbs and index finger together making a circle like on *Kung Fu* and *The Karate Kid*. Then very slowly he opened his eyes and said, "We're going to Tuscumbia."

"There are no monks or whatever you call yourself in Tuscumbia. No sir. But you go on ahead; I'll just stay right here. I'll help you get back in your suitcase and you can wiggle your nose or whatever you have to do to go to where you want to go."

"I'm going to Tuscumbia and you're coming with me."

"Tus-fucking-cumbia? I don't think so! Give me one good reason why I should."

"Once upon a time there was this man named Nasrudin. One night he went searching for something. A few hours later a Constable saw him on his hands and knees under a street lamp. The Constable said, 'What are you doing Nasrudin?' Nasrudin replied, 'I'm looking for something I lost,' and he continued his search. The Constable asked, 'Did you lose what you are looking for here?' pointing to the light pole. 'No,' Nasrudin said matter-of-factly. 'Then why are you looking here?' Nasrudin stopped his search for a moment and looked the Constable in the eye. 'Because the light is better here.'"

I stroked my face with both hands over and over like Curly does in the Three Stooges. "You're messing with my head again, ain't ya?"

"It means that Blue is the best thing your daddy ever gave you," he said while petting Blue. "Your grandfather is the only man you've ever trusted in your whole life. You have always thought you had a destiny to fulfill and it isn't here in Scottsboro and the Unclaimed Baggage. So let's go find it," he paused. "Should I go on?" He didn't wait for an answer. "We only have seven days to work this out. Be ready by sunrise."

"Why so early?"

Pooh smiled, as he pointed to the roof, "Like an old friend said once, 'The breeze at dawn has secrets to tell you.'"

# Chapter 5

I woke up early the next morning and Pooh was sitting on the floor with his index fingers touching his thumbs and making kind of a circle. I looked at him and saw a serene calm on his face that I'd never seen on anybody else's except my granddaddy's. He had the same look some mornings at breakfast after saying grace and pouring his coffee in his saucer and blowing on it to let it cool before taking a sip. My grandfather was just a sharecropper and a sharecropper's son. He was a man of few words, but he carried himself in a way that spoke loudly that he was at peace with himself and God. I always wanted that peace but just didn't know how to find it. I kept looking for it like my daddy did in the bottom of a beer can or whiskey bottle. As I watched Pooh I got to thinking that maybe he did have something to teach me. I didn't know what and I certainly didn't understand what was happening. I mean the whole suitcase thing, and him being from up there and this whole "the Wise Ones" seemed like a bunch of bullshit. But I also knew that there had to be something more than working for Skeeter at the Unclaimed Baggage and getting drunk and going frog giggin' with Chigger and arguing with my ex-wives and not ever talking to my son and hating my old man. I just didn't know what it was so what the hell. I decided to go with this nut job and see where we ended up and what would happen. This is how I always made decisions in my life.

About the time I was thinking all of this Pooh looked me straight in the eye and said, "I knew you would come around. Trust me. Now get packed and we are going to go to Tuscumbia, Alabama, to see that friend I was talking about." He had this shit-eatin' grin all over his face.

"All right, I'm going with you but lemme ask you a question. Why Tuscumbia, Alabama? It's two and a half hours from here and I don't think you can fit in my truck."

"Well, first, you'll see why Tuscumbia when we get there. Second, it's going to take more than two hours because of the way we are traveling, and third, I won't be riding in your truck. We are going to go by river. We'll take your truck and I'll ride in the back and we'll go catch a ride on what you people call a barge and towboat, which, my friend is plenty big enough for me to ride on. So let's get going."

"You got to be fuckin' kiddin' me. A barge! Why a barge? Have you ever been on one? Let me tell you I worked on one of those for a summer after graduation to make some money and barge work is some of the dirtiest, exhaustingest work a man can do."

"Don't worry. We'll get on. And you will pay our way by working and I'll find something to do. But that's how we are going to get there because the Wise Ones said so. So let's go."

I wrote Skeeter a note that I'd be gone for a while and if he needed to give my job and my room to someone else they'd be no hard feelings between us.

So I got in my pickup and he got in the back with empty beer cans and Blue. We went to the banks of the Tennessee River, where I knew from having worked that summer, they would pull in and let old crews off and take on new ones and supplies. You should have seen everyone staring at Pooh in the back of my little Toyota. It sagged to one side because he was so heavy. I called Chigger before we left and told him to meet us down at the dock so he could pick up Blue and take my truck and use it while I was gone with this wild man to who knows where and who knows why.

Chigger came roaring up on his army-camouflaged four-wheeler. His truck was broke down, which is why I was leaving him mine. Pooh and I were standing on the riverbank and Pooh was just staring into the water.

"Mornin' Bubba. What the hell are you doing here?" Chigger looked over at Pooh. "Who the hell is that?"

"I told you about him the other night at the pond. That's the crazy guy who owns the suitcase and who popped out of it."

"Man, you ain't got the sense God gave a billy goat. Nobody can come out of a suitcase. He must have tricked you somehow. Magicians know how to do all kind of shit," he said giving Pooh the once over.

"Well, all I know is he's here and somehow the son-of-a-bitch has talked me into taking a trip with him and I guess that's what I am gonna do. Go over there. Just touch him. You'll see. He's real."

"Man, I ain't touching nobody. Besides he might think I'm queer or something. I ain't going to be touching no man, but I am going to talk to him and you'll see I'll prove him for the joke he really is."

Chigger hiked up his britches, scratching his head while walking real slowly over to Pooh like he was sneaking up on a rattlesnake. Chigger's grandfather was a holiness minister over on Sand Mountain, and if anyone knew how to sneak up, old Chigger did.

"Hey you, One-Hung-Lo. What kind of a fast one are you trying to pull on my best friend here? He thinks you came out of a suitcase. I think he and you are full of shit. Where do you come from? I bet you escaped from some loony bin, either that or you're from San Francisco or New York, same thing in my opinion."

"Hello, Chigger, how's your mommanem? I love how you rednecks speak."

"My momma ain't none of your business, Mr. Con man. Besides how do you know my name? I ain't told you my name. I bet Bubba told you about me."

"I know lots of things—people's names, places they have been, places they need to go, and no, Bubba never told me about you."

"Well, if you know so goddamn much, I bet you think you know the secret of life don't you?"

Pooh looked Chigger right in his eyes and then over at me, "Yes, I do."

"Bullshit. You want me to think you know the answer so I'll look stupid and ask you what it is. All right, I'll bite—what is the secret to life?"

"Oh, I couldn't tell you that."

"And why the hell not?" Chigger sounded irritated.

"Because it's a secret."

Chigger threw up his hands and shook his head from side to side. "See, I knew you don't know shit from shinola. Bubba, if you go with this guy you are one crazy motherfucker."

Chigger made a fist and bumped mine, called to Blue and put him in the back and just as he did, old Blue started howling. I wasn't sure if it was because I was leaving or for his new best friend or if he just wanted some beer to go. Chigger got in the truck and peeled out all the while talking to himself. I got my suitcase and Pooh and I sat down on the riverbank and waited for the towboat to come pick us up and carry us to Tuscumbia.

"Pooh. I don't know who you are or what I'm doing here with your China ass, but I do want to know what makes you think the captain is going to let us on his boat. He doesn't know me and one look at you and he's going to think we are both touched in the head."

"Trust me. I know the captain. He'll let us on."

"Now how in the hell would you know the captain? I thought you just got here."

"Trust me. I know your mom loves cornbread and milk for dinner. I know your daddy was a good listener when he was sober. I know your second wife never really loved you and that Blue and Chigger are the only two friends you have besides me and that you're not nearly as dumb as you think you are. And I know that the best way you can make your dreams come true is by waking up."

"Damn that was a mouthful, and you keep my momma and her cornbread out of this."

We sat on the banks of the Tennessee River, which is one of the most beautiful sights a man can ever see. It winds through small mountains, the kind that don't overwhelm you. In the spring and summer, the vegetation on Sand Mountain's soft peaks shines like emeralds. And in the fall—that's my favorite time of year—the trees show off gold, purple, yellow, and red. The colors are so beautiful it makes you want to slap your momma. The river's water is a blue-green like a pretty woman's eyes, and I have loved it all my life. Christians are supposed to be buried in the ground, but someday I'm going to tell someone who loves me to burn me up and scatter my ashes right here in this river and let me just roll past Mobile Bay and flow on to the Gulf of Mexico.

As I sat there staring into the water I was already missing old Blue. Dogs know all kinds of things about people that people will never know, and Blue doesn't act like he did with this man with just anyone. I knew I was gonna miss him something terrible. I've always been glad Daddy gave him to me.

A few minutes later a squat, dirty-white towboat appeared, pushin' ten or twelve coal barges. The captain blew the horn and came straight for us. I still wasn't sure how this here thing was gonna work, but I was beginning to get it that Pooh, like Blue, knew some things I just didn't.

# Chapter 6

A deckhand threw a rope my way, and I tied it around a big live oak. A couple more lines were tossed and tied off. A young guy, who must have been one of the green hands on the towboat because of the awkward way he threw down the gangplank, got off with a couple of fellas. The plank was just barely wide enough for me to walk across to the boat.

Usually the captain rarely leaves the pilothouse except to sleep or eat. About half the time the cook sends his meals up to him with one of the deckhands, but this captain came down to where we were getting on. When he saw Pooh, his face lit up like the Fourth of July.

He was a pretty old guy with white, bushy hair and a mustache that was wide and covered his lips. A slight figure of a man, the captain was dressed in white pants, white shirt, and a white coat. He looked more like a riverboat captain than a towboat captain. He grabbed Pooh around his shoulders or at least as much as he could get of him with his wiry arms. Pooh kissed him on both cheeks and the captain didn't even mind! I figured he must not be from around these parts or he was a little light in his loafers, if you know what I mean.

"Captain Sam, how are you doing?" Pooh said. "It's been a long,

long time. I see you still love your river, as much as I did and still do. You may recall my time working on the ferry before I finally sat down."

"Yes, of course I remember. That's one of the great gifts the Wise Ones bestow on you. I recall most everything that matters. I'm so thankful." The captain looked like he was shedding a southern man's tear as he talked. You know, the kind that looks like something is in his eye but it ain't. And he wipes it away before anybody can see it.

"Well, you deserve it. That's your good karma working. You did great things. Unlike the doer of unkind, useless, or hurtful things, you not only get to come back and remember, you get to choose who and what you come back as. It's a good deal," Pooh said, patting the captain on the back real gentlelike.

"I decided to do my second great love since people don't read that much nowadays. Besides, I'm not sure my sense of humor would work these days. Okay, enough waxing nostalgic, let's get you and this boy where you're going and just let me say again how much gratitude I have for that time together all those years ago. I wouldn't have written a thing were it not for our journey together. By the way, is this your first time back since then?"

"It is. You're welcome, and I'm a little rusty. You'd think the Wise Ones would have given me an easier project than a dyed-in-the-wool redneck to bring me back up to speed. But then again, they know more than us put together." Pooh looked real serious and my feelings got hurt just a little when he said the thing about me being a redneck. It sounded like something bad when he said it. I didn't much understand anything else they were talking about.

"Good day, Sir. Welcome on board," the captain said to me as he was shaking my hand. "Ben Rogers, my first mate, will show you where to bunk. He'll put you to work straightaway. Pu Tai, you can bunk with me in the pilothouse. You'll only be a couple of nights before we get to Tuscumbia. Son, have you ever worked as a deckhand before?" he said, turning to me and lighting his cigar.

"Yes, Sir, I worked two tours after I graduated from high school to make me a little money for my wife and kid." I didn't tell him how I swore to myself I'd never work on a barge again as long as I lived.

Captain Sam just looked curiously at Pooh for a few minutes and then at me. "Well, let's get you fellas on your way."

The captain looked and sounded somewhat familiar. He wasn't from the Deep South. He sounded more like he was from the Ozarks. Most of the deckhands are good ol' boys from places like Paducah, Kentucky; Cairo, Illinois; Decatur, Alabama. They come out here on this river to work twenty-one days on and twenty-one days off. Most of the men are about as educated as I am or less. You'd have to be pretty hungry to work the shifts towboaters work. Six hours on, six hours off. You get up twice and go to bed twice. No sooner than your head hits the pillow, it's time to get up, grab a cup of coffee, eat a bite, and get back to work. And the work is hot and dirty in the summertime and cold and dirty in the wintertime. Time you wash off a little dirt and settle down in your bunk, listening to the constant hum of the engine pushing barges full of coal, corn, fertilizer, you maybe get three hours of sleep. Still, barges have always attracted attention because, stacked end to end, they're a good bit longer than the *Titanic* and forty something feet longer than an aircraft carrier. The money is pretty good for someone with only a high school education and beats the hell out of working at McDonalds or Hardees. The food is good—in fact, you'll never find better. You might find better-looking women to cook it, because companies won't hire anyone too pretty; it's just too distracting. Miss Watson, the cook on this towboat, the *Missouri*, is over two hundred pounds, got tattoos all over her body. The one on her right arm was a pitchfork with the words over it "The Devil Made Me Do It," and on the left arm was an anchor and over it were the "Semper Fi." She wears these little-bitty AC/DC and White Snake T-shirts that probably fit her in junior high (she later told me she was real skinny back then), but now the bottom of the shirt comes down just below her boobs and shows her big belly.

Captain Sam took Pooh right up to the pilothouse where he would be riding during the whole trip and sleeping even when the first mate was steering. One of the senior deckhands showed me my bunk and put me to work immediately sweeping out one of the barges that looks like a gray coffin that had been full of corn.

I hated going down into empty steel barges. Luckily for me it was April instead of July, but even then it was hot and spooky. As I was down there I kept wondering what in the hell I was doing. About all I could see that was in this for me was to lose some sleep, eat some good food, and watch the deckhands make fun of my traveling companion.

The first day was hell because of two older deckhands, brothers Tom and Joe Harper. Everyone called Tom "Skinny" because he's huge, and his brother, Joe, "Tater" because he only eats French fries, mashed potatoes, and hash browns. Both of them were giving the college kid a really hard time. I found out later he was taking off a semester to make some money. They kept calling him "Professor" even though he was only a freshman, and when they didn't call him that, they just called him "puke" or "college boy."

Skinny and Tater had to mess with both of us on account of me being new meat. The college boy and I would go to our bunks after each shift and find pictures of naked women or condoms filled up with air and tied like a balloon. College boy found some dead catfish under his pillow one morning, and I found my mattress lying in the floor. Pretty mild stuff, but it made getting to sleep very hard.

After I finished sweeping the barge, I sat on a bench just below the pilothouse window, which was open, and I heard Pooh and Captain Sam talking. The captain had some kind of weird radio station on, but I could hear both of their voices loud and clear.

"Why him and why now?" Captain said, over the woman's voice saying, "Welcome to the afternoon addition of 'Fresh Air.' My name is Terry Gross."

"The Wise Ones said it was him. I guess they chose him for the same reason as the others. He's more concerned with things than with people. His mind is closed. His heart is broken. He's asleep. He worries about everything under the sun. He worries about what he's going to get and not what he can give. Yes, he's the one."

"And how much time do you have?" asked Captain Sam.

"Seven days." It was the only time so far I'd heard his voice be anything other than calm.

Captain Sam held his cigar at arm's length and rolled it around in his fingers. "Is it the same deal as before?"

"Yes, it is. I sure hope I can do it in seven days, because the Wise Ones are always true to their word."

"Well, good luck, Pu Tai. You'll need it."

Before I had time to think about what they were saying, much less think about what "the one" meant, Ben Rogers, the first mate, came up and told me to clean the pilothouse—mop and dust and bring the captain some fresh sweet tea before I went to bed. By the time I got back with the tea the captain and Pooh had changed the subject.

"Captain Sam, exactly what does it mean, this term 'redneck'? How do you know if someone is a redneck unless they tell you?"

"That's pretty easy, Pu Tai. Let's see, originally, the term referred to a farmer because he worked out in the sun all day long in his cotton, corn, or soybean fields, and his neck was about the only thing that wasn't covered up. Back when I was a boy people used to wear long-sleeve shirts and wouldn't be caught dead in shorts or T-shirts working on a farm. Now 'redneck' has come to mean several things, stereotypically speaking. Most rednecks will have at least one old rusted-out car on blocks in the front yard of their trailer. They tend to drive pickup trucks, with a gun rack. They throw their dog, and a bunch of empty beer cans in the back. It might have oversized tires or raised white letters and probably dragging behind it a big bass-fishing boat. All the radio stations are set to country music and he knows where Johnny Cash and Merle Haggard served time and what Willie Nelson's middle name is. They wear cowboy boots, either lizard or snake skin, a belt with their name on the back in big white letters like those on their truck tires. Should I go on?"

"No, I got a real honest-to-Buddha redneck on my hands." He looked over at me and winked.

I knew they were making fun of my particular lifestyle, but I didn't care. Besides the description was accurate, even if I didn't have a belt with my name on it. So I kept cleaning while they just listened to the educational program on the radio the whole time. After I cleaned up the pilothouse I went down to the galley and had some coffee with ole Jim the engineer.

Jim was the only one on board who graduated from college, maybe with the exception of Captain Sam.

"So what's your name, son? And what are you doing out here with us riffraff?"

"They call me Bubba. I've worked on barges before. I'm just working on this one to pay for me and the big man to be taken to Tuscumbia for some reason. I'm not really sure why exactly."

"Is that heavy-set gentleman a friend of yours?"

"Well, I wouldn't say that exactly. I don't really know him that well."

"So why are you going somewhere with someone you don't even know?" ole Jim took a few puffs on his pipe.

"You got me."

"Do you know where he hails from?"

"You wouldn't believe me if I told you. Let's just say he popped in on me a couple of nights ago. I think he gets around a lot."

I guess I should mention here that ole Jim is a black man, or an African-American. I'm not real sure what he might want to be called these days. Growing up, my daddy and granddaddy always used the "N" word or "colored." I know enough to know they don't appreciate that much. My great-grandma on my daddy's side said, "Colored people were meant to be slaves and that it said so in the Bible and who didn't ever believe word for word the Bible was going to hell." If I could, I'd look her in the eye and tell her hell was where I'd rather be, because I don't believe that was true and even a redneck like me has the right to disagree. I guess in part 'cause I always felt like a slave to my daddy the way he made me work in the fields ever since I was six years old.

Whatever he is called, he sure is in the minority out here on the river. He's the only black man I've ever seen working on towboats. Jim has real dark skin and is bald as an eagle. His white T-shirt was almost as black as he was what from the engine oil and grease.

"Can I ask you a question?"

"Sure you can ask. I doubt that I'll know the answer but we'll give it a shot. What's on your mind?" Jim emptied his burnt tobacco out in his hands.

"Do you know what a Buddhist is? Or what they believe? Or really just anything 'cause I don't know nothing about them."

"I took a few religion courses in college. Why you so interested in a thing like that?"

"That big guy I'm traveling with, I bet you anything he is

one of them Buddhists, though he ain't said so."

"Pour us a couple cups of coffee and we'll begin the class."

I got up and thought for about a minute what my friends, like Chigger, would say if they saw me getting ole Jim a cup of Joe and trying to learn anything from him.

"So here's how she goes. The Buddha was this man, like you or me, except he lived in one of the heavens." He pointed up just like Pooh would do. "Well, he came down to earth to preach. He was born to a queen and they gave him a funny-sounding name to us—Siddhartha, although he has been called many names. It was predicted by someone, I can't rightly say who, that he would be a wise man and he would turn his back on the things of this world if he ever saw sickness, old age, or death. His father and mother tried to shield him from ever seeing these things. But he saw them anyway and walked away from his father's palace and all his inheritance to go live in the woods with these other guys who had renounced everything. He meditated, fasted, prayed, and chanted all the things Buddhists still do today. He even worked on the river for a while on a ferryboat taking people from shore to shore. He married and had a son as I recall. Finally out of depression and discouragement for not being able to feel satisfied he just sat down one day under a Bodhi tree by the river—probably a river like this—and he was determined to sit there until something happened because he was tired."

"That's it?"

"There's a lot more, but I got to get back to Big Bertha and see how she's doing. You better get some sleep. You have to pull another six-hour shift in about four more hours."

"Who is Big Bertha?"

"Oh," he said smiling. "That's what I call this old engine of mine."

I lay there later that night in my bunk listening to the steady hum of the engines underneath me. I stared at the slats on the bunk bed above me as I tossed and turned and kept waking up. The slats reminded me of the corrugated ridges in the barge I had cleaned out that day. I had about a dozen dreams where I was in those barges, closed up tight, confined, and I kept trying to escape. I'd wake up for a minute and realize I was in my bunk, but it was a horrible few hours before they got me up to go to work again.

As I was drinking my coffee trying to wake up, I kept thinking how everything is backasswards from the way it should be. The *Missouri* is called a towboat but it pushes shit up and down the river—it doesn't tow it. It looks like a ship cut in half lashed to barges with hundreds of feet of steel cable an inch thick—scissor wires, jockey wires, fore-and-afts all tightly wired to one another, and boy hidey, I ain't kiddin' ya the ratchets used to keep these things together is heavier than hell and the green hands have to tote them and tighten the wires together. If one of those wires snaps or if you fall off in between barges, that's the end of you. Right at that moment I hated the work and I hated Pooh, Buddhists, barges, and everything else. I couldn't remember why I was here until Ben thumped me on the ear and snapped me out of it and pissed me off even more than I already was.

"You going to sit on your redneck ass all morning? You're burning daylight. You and college boy get out the head and tighten up those wires all the way back here. If I see you boys jerking each other off out there I'll throw your asses in the Tennessee River."

Ben Rogers was a mean son-of-a-bitch if there ever was one. He had tattoos all over him, even more than the cook, Miss Watson, and that's saying something. He wore old, black Harley Davidson T-shirts, black jeans, and black cowboy boots. Hell, everything about him was black except his skin—hair was black, and eyes as dark as the coal the *Missouri* was pushing that morning to Decatur. He was fit as a fiddle and about as tightly wound. He was the kind of man you didn't want to mess with but wanted on your side if push came to shove.

College boy and I walked out to the head of the tow. I looked back and could see the pilot, John Canty, who is the opposite of Captain Sam. The captain listened to classical music or jazz, Canty listened to nothing but old-time country classics like Hank Williams and Ferlin Husky and those guys. He chain smoked cigarettes and cussed everybody out anytime he wanted to, except the captain, of course. His face was always red like a beet. I think it was because he drank a lot of whiskey when he was off shift but because he never seemed drunk no one seemed to give a good goddamn. Anyway, he had this shit-eatin' grin on his face, and I wanted to shoot him the bird, but I didn't want to get on his bad side. I still had a couple of days to go, and when Captain Sam was asleep Canty could do anything he wanted to anybody he wanted.

The roar of the water passing under the barges was all you could hear. We were so far from the towboat we couldn't even hear the engines.

The college boy looked like he belonged back on campus, the way he was dressed and all. His crew cut, Gap T-shirt, and Levis said he probably belonged to a fraternity, which didn't make sense 'cause all them guys got daddies with lots and lots of money. I thought maybe he was in R.O.T.C.

"You got a name besides 'college boy' don't ya?" I asked.

"Harney Shepherdson. Where are you from?"

"I'm from Scottsboro, where me and the Oriental guy got on."

"I think they prefer to be called Asians. I mean no disrespect but you don't see many Asians in the South, except maybe over in Huntsville but certainly not on a towboat."

"I'd never met one before now. I'm mostly just along for the ride to see how this all plays itself out. You know what I mean, dude?" I thought I'd try talking less like a redneck around Harney since he'd been to college and all. He was about twenty years or so younger, but I liked him better than anyone on the boat so far except maybe ole Jim. He kinda reminded me of my son a little.

"So Harney, what is college like?"

"Lots of parties, pussy, and beer."

"Man, that sounds like the life to me. Why did you leave all of that to come out here to work?"

"Truth is, but don't tell any of the other guys, that I got suspended for a semester for flunking all of my courses the first two semesters and my dad said he wouldn't pay for school anymore. That's why I'm out here busting my ass so that when they let me back in I'll have some money to pay for books and tuition."

"But why towboats?"

"I'll tell you something else if you promise not to say anything."

"Promise, cross my heart, and hope to die. But not any time soon."

"My dad owns the company, but I'm not supposed to tell anybody."

"Wow! Fuck me. Your daddy owns this boat?"

"Yeah, and about twenty others all up and down the Tennessee, Mississippi, and Ohio rivers."

"Damn, your daddy's rich, and I bet your momma's good lookin' too!"

"What's your story?"

"I shrugged. I'll tell you if you tell me what you know about that fancy-dressed Captain Sam."

"Nothing I'm afraid. He's brand new, just got on a few days ago.

Seems like he had been on vacation or something. Sort of came out of nowhere. That's all I've got, now spill."

I gave him the highlights of my life until now. "I'm basically what you'd call a slacker. I'm too lazy to work and too scared to steal, so mostly I just go from job to job." I started working for my cousin over at Unclaimed Baggage and a few days ago this big Oriental guy," Harney looked at me funny, "I mean Asian man popped into my life and said I was supposed to go with him on a trip. I guess we're on what you'd call the first leg of it."

"So you mean to tell me this dude comes in from nowhere and you give up everything and take off with a stranger." I nodded. "Man you either got some steel ones or you're fucking insane."

"Insane, likely. But there's got to be something more than what I've been doing. You got to think that or you wouldn't be going to college. Isn't that what that's supposed to be about—learning stuff so you don't have to work out here or in a store unpacking other people's stuff? Am I right?"

About this time Ben's voice came over the bullhorn. "You boys gonna bump your gums all day long? All I want to see is asses and elbows down on those ratchets tightening those wires."

# Chapter 7

When Harney and I got back to the boat, Pooh was sitting on the bench below the pilothouse window. His eyes were closed and he had his first finger and thumb together like I'd seen before. There was a blissful look on his fat, buttery face as the breeze from the river gently rustled through his silk robe. I didn't want to interrupt whatever he was doing, but he opened his eyes and smiled.

"So how is your work, Bubba?"

"Let's put it this way. I'm glad we're just going a few miles down the river. If I'm not getting too personal I'd like to ask you a question."

"I'd be happy to answer."

"What are you doing?"

"You mean right now or in the big picture of things?"

"Right now. With your fingers and thumb and eyes shut." I asked.

"It's called meditation."

"Yeah, I've seen it on movies and TV. My favorite actor, Steven Seagal, does it a lot on his movies right before he breaks somebody's arm or kicks their ass. But what is it exactly?"

"Meditation is different things to different people, but mostly it's breathing, watching the breathing, and letting the things that come into the mind, come and not be attached to them and let them go."

"You mean it's sort of like catch-and-release fishing?"

Pooh smiled. "It is a practice of using right effort, right mindfulness, and right contemplation."

"Fuck me. I don't understand half of what you just said any more than I do the catch-and-release thing. I mean why would you throw a good fish back into the creek? I think you will have to explain it to me again sometime."

"Maybe someday I will teach you how to meditate."

"Thanks for the offer but for the meantime I'll just settle for a peaceful spot on the river bank or take my Crimson Tide folding chair out by a pond and a fishing pole and watch the water, and listen to the birds and frogs and such."

"You understand perfectly. Maybe sometime you will take me to that special spot and you'll teach me—how do you say it?—to drown a worm."

About this time one of the older deckhands, a guy they called Big Dick (though his real name was Hugo Hendon) came up and started messin' with Pooh. Hugo sort of nicknamed himself "Big Dick" because one day a green deckhand said to him, "You know, you're just a big dick." And Hugo thought he said that he had a big dick and took it as a compliment and that's how it got started. I didn't know the story about his real name until later, but I know he is the kind of guy that gives rednecks a bad name. People confuse us with "white trash," which is different than a redneck or a cracker. Big Dick is white trash. He don't take a bath but about every blue moon or so, and lord knows he's irritating and ugly, both in his behavior and his outlook on life. Big Dick is the kind of guy who has about a dozen coon dogs tied up in the backyard and beats the hell out of them and doesn't feed them worth a shit, whups the hell out of his children and wife, and is just plain nasty talking, and oh yeah, a racist—the kind that makes up the worst part of the South—the Klan.

"What are you doing with this fat chink?" Big Dick was looking at me with tobacco running down his chin.

"Go on Big. Leave us be."

"Fuck you and the horse you rode in on. The captain is asleep and I'm asking you a question. What are you doing with this yellow China man?"

Pooh took a deep breath and let it out real slow like.

"Does that make you mad, Chink?"

I didn't know what was going to happen. Big Dick stands over six feet and weighs about two hundred and something pounds. The Dick got angrier the longer Pooh didn't say anything back.

"I believe you are traveling with a pussy, Bubba. Are you a pussy too? Maybe you both are faggot, fudge packers. Yeah, that's it—you're queer for each other."

I started getting real angry about this time, but I didn't want any trouble and if something got started Captain Sam would probably put us off his boat in the middle of nowhere.

"Pussy, fudge-packing queers," he repeated.

Pooh took two or three deep breaths and stood up and looked the man straight in the eyes and just stared at him but not harshly, more like the way a mother looks at a little baby that was sick or hurting. I thought fists would start flying, but I saw the damn'dest thing. Pooh raised his hand and pointed it in Big's direction and just went "Shhhhh" and Big Dick tucked his head down and took a step back and went back into the galley, never saying a word or nothing. I was stunned plum speechless.

"Pooh, what the hell just happened? I thought you and that piece of white trash was going to tie into each other. How did you do that?"

"Oh, you mean the shhhh thing? It's an old technique for turning bad dogs into good ones. You ever seen the Dog Whisperer?"

"The what?"

"Never mind. He was just one of TWOS' better students. Maybe someday you will meet him."

Most of the time I didn't know what the hell Pooh was talking about, and this was another case in point. I went to work my shift for six hours. We had to break the tow down 'cause the towboat *Decatur* was going upriver and we swapped loads. I told Harney about what happened. I kept thinking about it the whole shift. After I got off my watch I saw Pooh sitting underneath the pilothouse window again and I was worn plum out, but I had to ask him why he was looking so damn peaceful after what had happened earlier that day.

"Why aren't you still pissed at Big Dick, Pooh? Hell, I would be. That ignorant son-of-a-bitch pisses me off just thinking about the way he talked to me and you."

"Bubba, let me tell you a story." He started walking with his hands folded in front of him like he was about to pray. "One time there was an old monk and a young monk who were making a pilgrimage from the monastery to a holy place, miles away. The two of them came up to a huge mud puddle and standing there was this beautiful young woman. Now monks take a vow to never touch women and both monks knew this well. The old monk looked at the woman, then looked at the puddle and he picked the woman up and put her on his back and carried her across and set her down on the other side. The two monks continued their journey. At the end of a long day the monks retired for the night. The young monk said, 'You know it is not permissible for monks to touch women and yet you picked that woman up and carried her across the mud puddle. How could you do that? It is part of the vows we take.' The old monk responded, 'I left her on the other side of the puddle; have you not been carrying her all day?'"

Now I guarandamtee you I didn't understand the story. Well, maybe just a little. I think what Pooh was saying is that what had happened in that moment between Big Dick and him was over and there was no need chewing your cud for a second time.

But I knew I had to try to get a few more minutes with ole Jim the engineer and find out a little bit more about this Buddhist stuff. So after another six hours of working my dick in the dirt cleaning two more barges, I went to get me a shower and find Jim. He was in the galley drinking coffee and Miss Watson was busy making her world-renowned cinnamon rolls, which she served on Sundays. Today was Saturday. Let me tell you Sunday on a towboat is some of the best eating a man can do. I mean fried chicken, mashed potatoes, green beans, fried green tomatoes. Boy, you almost feel like all that back-breaking work was worth it.

Anyways there was Jim, puffing on a roll-your-own cigarette sittin' in the booth where all the deckhands take their meals. The galley is about as big as some rich person's bathroom with stainless-steel cupboards and appliances lining three of the walls. There's also a large iron cooker that looks like a witch's brew-pot bolted to the floor in the center of the room. All the kitchen utensils are clipped to the wall so they won't fall when the weather gets rough. When you first walk in, the smell of the cooked food welcomes you like a long-lost love. Even though there aren't any windows, you feel free.

"Tell me some more about them Buddhist people." I thought about telling him about the incident with Pooh and Big Dick but thought better of it.

"Well, about the only other thing I know is that this ole Buddha taught his followers that there are four facts of life. The first one is that life itself is full of suffering. But here's what's interesting.

The Buddha didn't think there was some god in the sky making us suffer as a way to punish us." Jim took a drag off his cigarette.

"In other words, it ain't a trip to the woodshed."

"Suffering is just a part of life. I guess he came to this after he saw those sights his momma and daddy tried to keep from him. You know, death, disease, old age, and such. The second fact of life as the Buddha sees it is that the culprit for all this suffering is from us wanting and craving so much from this world that we tie ourselves all up in knots trying to get it. There was this old poet from London, England, who said, 'Getting and spending we lay waste to our powers and little in nature do we see that is ours.'"

I looked at him funny.

"Anyway, I digress. The third thing Buddha tried to teach is that if a man could stop craving so much and wanting so much the suffering could come to an end. The last one is that if you want to stop desiring so much, then you practice what he called the Noble Eight Fold Path. So there you go. What do you think about that?"

"What little of it I understand sounds good enough. I know he's right about that life is full of sufferin'. But the rest of it I'll have to study on for a while I reckon. I ain't never seen anybody who didn't have a powerful cravin' for stuff. I remember one time my momma wanted a new couch so bad I thought she was gonna swap me for it at trade day over in Collinsville. This fella had a brand-new one and he wanted fifty dollars for it. I don't know where the money came from, but she bought it and she kept the plastic on it for three or four years, which is terrible sticky in the summertime when she let us sit on it. And my daddy craved liquor even more than I do, and I know he would have swapped me for a gallon of white lightning before he would have went bone dry. I want and want and wish I had more all the time. I appreciate you telling me this stuff. Can you tell me about the eight-fold thing before we get to Tuscumbia?"

"Son, I think you'll have to get your traveling companion to explain that because we're going to be in Tuscumbia late tomorrow, and I don't think we'll have time. Besides, I couldn't do it justice." He pulled out a book he had on his lap under the table and began reading. I think it said the Koran on it or something like that.

I lay in my bunk thinking about the craving stuff and the suffering stuff until I went to sleep. I had this weird dream that I beat up my daddy and as I was hitting him he turned into Big Dick and as I beat up Big Dick he turned back into my daddy and they kept doing this back and forth. Finally, right before I woke up to the sound of Harney's voice telling me it was time to get up, I realized it was my face on Big Dick's body and my daddy's face on my body.

I had to get to work to pull my next-to-last shift, which, let me tell you, wasn't a good one.

# Chapter 8

It was about five in the morning and the sun hadn't even gotten up yet when the *Missouri* and fifteen barges lost speed and came to a quick stop. A twelve-hundred-and-forty-five-foot vessel had run aground. The port wing wire had snapped first, followed by seven or eight other wires. When wires snap they sound like cannons shooting. The port wing wire runs from the last barge in the port string to the towboat. It and the one in front of it started slowly sliding off on its own downriver. Canty, who was ending his shift, sounded the general alarm, which is loud enough to wake the dead. Luckily at this time of the day all the hands were up because it was time to change the watch. The space between the grounded vessel and the two barges that got loose widened.

Ben ran up with a line that had an eye in one end and tried to lasso a steel cavil on the barge. He only had one chance. Ben threw and the line fell short and dropped into the water. The barges drifted farther away. Captain Sam threw the throttle in reverse on the portside engine. The reversed wheel wash created some kind of wave or something. Now don't ask me how, but something unexplainable happened. The two barges stopped cold and they turned around and started drifting back towards us as we stood there with our mouths open. Ben made another lasso attempt and this time he hooked her and then the other one. We got them all back together. That's when me and Big Dick got into it.

It's scary as hell out here anytime of the year 'cause certain things can happen in a minute. Like for instance what happened while Big Dick and I were out on the barges tightening the ratchets trying to get everything back together again. There was created what towboaters call a "duck pond," which is an open space amongst the barges where a crewmember could fall in. There had been one created because of "oddball barges" not coming together smoothly and tightly and Big Dick and I were working right near one.

Big Dick looked pissed off about something. I wasn't sure if it was at the barges or at me. I found out pretty quick it was me.

"I don't know what kind of hoodoo your fat Chink friend put on me earlier, but he's not around to do it now and I think you and he are queers and we don't take to queers out here on the river and not only that we all saw you talking to nigger Jim. White men don't talk to him. So are you a nigger-lover on top of being a queer?" He started coming towards me with the knife in his hands that nearly all seasoned deckhands have attached to their belts. "So I'm going to slice your dick off. What do you think about that, you little pussy?"

Shit fire and save the matches! I didn't know if he was kiddin' or what. He sure didn't look like he was. "Listen here you piece of inbred white trash, you take that shit back. There ain't no call to talk like that about Pooh, Jim, or me, you son-of-a-bitch." I was backing up towards the duck pond, and I don't mind telling you I was scared stiff.

"You don't talk about my mother, you little shit." His face was turning as red as a tomato. I knew I either had to fight him, fuck him, or faint on him 'cause I wasn't going in the river to be pulled right under the barges and into the propeller. I decided I'd go down fighting.

So I ran towards him and away from the duck pond and tackled him. We both went down and started wrestling around bumping into all kind of shit. We looked like two schoolboys on a playground, not like the way men fight in the movies or TV. I was hitting him anywhere I could find and he was doing the same, both of us calling each other names. We were wrestling more than fighting and he dropped his knife, thank God. Neither one of us got in a good lick before Captain Sam called out over the loudspeaker to stop. Ben pulled us apart. He walked us back to the pilothouse, where the captain was waiting.

"Boys, I don't allow this on my boat. I don't give a darn, which one of you started it but I'm going to end it. We're coming into Wilson Dam lock this afternoon, and Hugo, get your belongings. You'll be getting off early and you can come back on next time. Bubba, son, I'm going to put you and Pooh off there as well. It wouldn't be right to let you stay on after the fight and ya'll will be able to get a ride to Tuscumbia from there. It's only about twelve miles or so. You boys can go, but if you give me more trouble I'll put you off right on the bank and you can walk."

Captain never raised his voice. He looked at me and said, "Come on in to the pilothouse. I want to talk to you a minute." He pulled out a cigar and offered me one. "I have made it a rule never to smoke more than one cigar at a time. Truth is, if there are no cigars in Heaven, I shall not go." He stared out the window. He went on, "Son, let me give you some advice for the rest of your trip with Pu Tai and the rest of the trip of your life: Love your enemy; it will scare the hell out of them."

"Huh," was all I said.

"I know you think you are just a dumb redneck hillbilly be-

cause of the way you've been brought up, but don't let school inter-
fere with your education. Anyone who can only think of one way
to spell a word obviously lacks imagination. It is obvious to me and
Pu Tai you are smart and don't lack imagination or you wouldn't be
out here with him on this trip. So listen to him."

The captain puffed on his cigar for about a minute or two.
"Some things you can just tell about a man. You have the look of a
father who wasn't fathered very well and is afraid he'll do the same
to his son."

"How do you know I have a son, Captain?"

"Some things you can just tell. We are always too busy for our
children; we never give them the time or interest they deserve. We
lavish gifts upon them; but the most precious gift, our personal as-
sociation, which means so much to them, we give grudgingly."

I thought that sounded real smart. Captain Sam sure had a way
with words.

"That was right of you to stand up for yourself, your friend, and
ole Jim out there. You take care of yourself now and listen well."

I left the pilothouse in a daze and went off to get my stuff ready
to leave.

I saw Pooh and Captain Sam talking in the pilothouse. They
were both laughing and smiling and hugging, shaking hands, kissing each other on the cheeks. It was a little embarrassing. I'd never
seen men carry on like such and thought they ought to get a room
or something.

Pooh took his place on the bench under the pilothouse window and was meditating again, and I just watched from a good
distance 'cause I didn't want to disturb him. After about ten or
fifteen minutes he took his index finger and curved it with a come-
here gesture without even opening his eyes. I knew right away he
was motioning me to come, but I didn't know how he knew I was

down on the first barge watching him. When I got up there he opened his eyes.

"Pooh, I'm sorry about getting us throwed off the boat before we got to Tuscumbia, but I couldn't let stand what he was saying about me out there awhile ago and what he said about us both earlier." My voice was quivering a little bit and I didn't know why.

"It's okay, Bubba. You worry too much." His voice was calm.

"If I weren't such a peckerwood and he wasn't such white trash maybe I could have just walked away or tried that 'shhhhh' thing you did with him."

"Let me ask you a question. Do you think it was the right action to take?" Pooh just stared into the sky, waiting for my answer.

"Hell, how do I know? It was what I was taught to do in situations like that one. If a man calls you a name or insults your momma, you're supposed to defend yourself and your good name. What another man would have done I can't rightly say."

"Well, it is only for you to say. Taking the right action at the right time is something each individual has to determine for himself." Pooh never stopped looking at the sky.

"Well, Jesus would have turned the other cheek I guess. If I were a good Christian fella I guess I'd done that. Is that what you're saying?" I was getting a little frustrated and my brain was starting to hurt from all this thinking that I wasn't in the practice of doing.

"Maybe that would have been the right action for him. I'll have to ask him the next time I run into him, but right now I can't say. Just like I can't say what is the right thing for you. You and only you can say. I can say that the way Hugo was brought to think the way he does is not the right way to think about people. Now don't worry about getting us put off. Captain Sam and I are fine friends and nothing can stop that. Besides, he said there is a wonderful Marriott hotel right there by the dam. He called ahead and arranged accommodations. We'll get a room there for the night and continue our journey to Tuscumbia in the morning."

"How we gonna pay for a room at that fancy hotel? I don't have that kind of money."

Without a moment's pause Pooh said, "See, that's what I'm talking about. You worry too much. Remember what Jesus said, 'Consider the lilies of the field, they neither toil nor spin.' Captain Sam said he would pay you for the two days and he'd take it out of his pocket and get reimbursed by the company later."

I worked one more shift and said my good-byes to everybody except the asshole I got into it with. The sky was beautiful and heartbreaking at the same time. The damp air whipped at my face and I was feeling like I was leaving someplace important, although I couldn't wait to get off the barge.

Everybody said they were glad to have met me and worked with me and they was glad I stood up for myself against Big Dick, which right after the tussle they all started calling him little Dick just to piss him off. When I went down to the engine room where I could barely hear myself think I told Jim good-bye and he said something I'll never forget, even though I've heard it a thousand times. "Don't judge a book by its cover."

I helped the fellas lock through the dam. As they pushed on downriver, Pooh and I watched for a few minutes but didn't say anything. Everybody waved and looked at us enviously as we got off the boat. I was looking forward to taking the money Captain Sam gave me, which came to a hundred and twenty something dollars and getting a nice room. I'd never stayed in anything much except motels. As we were standing on the dam watching the boat slip down closer to the purple horizon, I noticed Pooh's eyes were watery.

He looked at me and said, "Have you ever seen anything so

beautiful in your whole life? This is one of the most sacred spots I've ever been to."

"Pooh, it's just a river in Alabama. You've been everywhere from what I could see of that suitcase I hallucinated you popping out of. Do you really think it's that special?" I started looking at the view real hard like, shuttin' one eye and cocking my head at different angles tryin' to see what he was seein'. It was just a pretty sunset over water, wasn't it? Could it be that I'd looked at this river all my life and yet had never seen it?

"Trust me. It was special to Cherokees and Choctaws long before the dam was built, and it's just as sacred, beautiful, and holy now. Right now it is the only place in the world I want to be, and you are the only person I'd like to be seeing it with. It's the right view."

I guess I never really considered all the different people that had sailed through here and raised their families near this river. What was so special about this place that made them sacrifice and build a life here? I closed my eyes for a second, and when I opened them again, the sky had turned from gold to dark blue. Then I realized I'd missed sunsets all my life and as soon as I thought that, I also thought I missed my own son all my life.

I turned to Pooh and thought about telling him about all them feelings welling up inside me about Lucius. My mouth opened slightly, but I got too nervous to form words. Pooh seemed to read my mind and just nodded slowly as if he understood. I tried real hard not to get emotional—good thing I had a lot of practice with that.

Finally, he broke the silence and said, "Let's get a room."

# Chapter 9

Boy hidey you should see that hotel—fancy! They have this big ol' aquarium in the lobby and shiny marble floors and everyone says, "Good afternoon, sir," and "Yes, sir," and "No, sir." But there was one problem that I figured was gonna mess it all up. The woman behind the counter smiled at Pooh and me when we stepped up to it to get our room.

"Good evening, sir, how are you this beautiful night?" the lady said. "I believe you are the gentlemen Captain Sam called about. We have a reservation for a beautiful room that overlooks the river. He requested a king-size bed." The desk lady said so politely like she'd been raised in the South, but with a Yankee accent.

I pulled Pooh's arm and motioned for him to step back. "Pooh she said a king-size bed. What about my room?"

"Do you have enough money to pay for another room?"

"No sir. You know I don't."

Pooh paused and smiled, "Then I guess we'll have to make do with the one." He winked at me, "Trust me."

Now I got to tell you this was going a little too damn far for me. Everybody knows that when two women have to share a room there ain't no problem and no one necessarily is going to think they are from Lesbovia. Women can do that sort of stuff and get away with it just fine. But men, all men—not just us rednecks—are taught from the day we were born that it ain't even right to get in your momma and daddy's bed even if you're scared when you're little, let alone sleep in the same bed with another full-grown man. So I took a coin out of my pocket and said to Pooh, "I'll flip you for the bed. Heads you get the bed and tails I get the bed. Whoever loses can either sleep in the bathtub or on the floor."

"All right, if you insist. The bed should be large enough to accommodate both of us." Pooh was grinning. I didn't see the humor in the situation.

"Yeah, but your big ass is gonna take up damn near all of it, and besides I ain't sleepin' with nobody that ain't a woman and you ain't one, so call it."

Damn if he didn't get the bed. But boy hidey were the rooms ever something. The shower was separate from the bathtub, which was where I'd be sleeping. The damn bathroom was bigger than my room at Unclaimed Baggage and even had a telephone in it. They had big acorns on the curtains and carpets and one of them flat-screen TVs with them kind of movies that me and Chigger would watch in secret when we were kids. When his mom was at the market, we'd run to the basement and turn on his momma's old projector. We watched those girly movies while eating candy bars and drinking whiskey. I thought I'd done died and gone to heaven.

Pooh planted his butt on the bed right off and patted the mattress with his left hand and then he closed his eyes. I thought he was going to take a nap or something. But he didn't. "Sit down, Bubba, and let me ask you a question before I meditate. And you are welcome to get in bed anytime that bathtub gets too uncomfortable, but here's the question. I want to know what you think the good things are about being raised in this part of the world."

"The good things? Well, I'll have to ponder on that for a few minutes. I'm sure there are some. Let's see." I thought for about five minutes and Pooh just lay there with his eyes closed. "All right then, here's a few: We never forget our momma and daddy's birthdays. Hell, I remember daddy's and he didn't hardly amount to anything in my life. We are taught always to say, 'Yes, sir,' and 'No, ma'am,' especially to people we don't know. We even say it to people younger than us and even to black folks. Us rednecks go see their kids play sports no matter what kind it is—wrestling matches, girls basketball—you name it. Our mommas know how to make the best biscuits and gravy and fried chicken in the whole damn world. We know not to tell someone we're going to do something unless we're going to do it, because our word is our bond. There you go. I can come up with more examples if you like."

Pooh opened his eyes. "Thank you, maybe you can tell me more later." He patted the bed again. "Sure you don't want to join me up here?"

"I'm real sure."

So I put the extra blanket and the comforter from the bed in the bathtub and got in thinking what if I had won the toss, Pooh wouldn't be able to fit in the bathtub and what would we have done then? So I got to studying about what he said about taking the right actions and the right view and what would have been the right thing. I drifted off to sleep and I had a bunch of dreams—mostly about my son, Lucius. Like I said earlier, I guess he'd be about twenty or twenty-one. I forget exactly what year he was born. Rednecks may remember their momma and daddy's birthday, but most of us forget our children's and even our own most of the time.

In one dream, Lucius and I were riding a military vehicle. I don't rightly remember where we were going, but it felt like we were in a war zone. I was driving and drinking, and my son, who is a little over six feet tall and got hands the size of hams and is wiry like me and his granddaddy, started beating me over the head with one of the empty beer bottles I'd thrown in the floorboard. He just kept hitting me and cursing me. "You son-of-a-bitch, why did you leave me? I hate your goddamn guts, old man." He was crying and carrying on, and I didn't say anything.

I woke up and realized where I was, and I hate to admit it but my eyes were leaking pretty good. Now don't get me wrong, I ain't no crybaby. I looked out into the room to make sure Pooh didn't hear me or see me. He was sleeping like a big boy dog. I got back in my bathtub and went to sleep again and I'll be damned if I didn't have another dream. I ain't never remembered any of my dreams before and now all of a sudden I'm remembering them right regular like. In this one I was in a prison and I was behind bars looking out and there was no other prisoners there exceptin' for me. But now here's the weird thing. I looked over and saw this guard and he had my face! The warden came walking towards me standing there in a black suit and damned if he didn't have my face, too. Then this priest with a Bible was looking at me and he had my face. I don't mind telling you this scared the ever-lovin' shit out of me. Finally, I pushed against the cell door and it flung wide open. I reckon I wanted out of there. Come to find out it wasn't even locked. The guard, priest, and warden started singing, "You can check in anytime you want, but you can never leave," and when they did they sounded just like the Eagles. The warden said, "But you could have left anytime you wanted, it's always been open." And here's the terrible thing about the dream. I turned around and went back in and shut the door behind me and took out the key I had in my pocket and stuck my arm through the door with it and locked it and gave the key to the guard, and he handed it to the warden and then he handed it to the priest and he handed it back to me and I stuck it in my pocket again and woke up sobbing like a little baby. Then I got up and went and got in bed with Pooh. Don't get me wrong—I stayed way over on my side and went sound to sleep.

The next morning Pooh was up sitting on the balcony doing his meditation thing and I made some coffee and asked Pooh if he wanted me to heat some water for his tea. He told me no but that he might have some later. I sat down and we both looked at the tall pines and the river. I wondered why I had never really looked at the trees and the river and some other things the way I was starting to look at them. The moon was still visible as was the sun, so it was still pretty early. Pooh said, "Bubba," as he pointed his finger at the moon. "This finger pointing to the moon is not the moon."

I looked at his finger and then I looked at the moon. "Pooh, what in the hell does that mean? Is that some Buddhist stuff?"

Pooh looked at me and smiled. "Trust me. You'll figure it out one of these days. Tell me about you and your son."

"How do you know about my son?" I had never mentioned him and I was stunned to say the least.

"You dreamed about him last night, didn't you?"

"How do you know?" Pooh was making me nervous. He was getting a little close to home, if you know what I mean.

"They sent you those dreams." He pointed to the sky. "Sometimes we dream things on our own and sometimes they send them."

"Well, we don't know each other well enough for me to talk about such things. It's personal. But I will tell you this; I can fix anything with an engine. I know how to skin animals, plant gardens, milk a cow, hoe acres of cotton, and how to be alone real well, but telling complete strangers about my personal business, well I don't know how to do that or even if a body should do that. I mean it's not like you're a shrink. Besides shrinks are just for crazy people and I'm not crazy. I may have lost my damn mind going off somewheres with you to who knows where and who knows why, but let's just forget the whole dream thing and go get some breakfast."

We went down to the cafe and shit fire was it ever swanky. The tables were covered with clean, white tablecloths, and there were fresh flowers in little fru fru vases on every table. The plates looked better than my momma's special china that she only uses for holidays. There was an all-you-can-eat buffet like nothing I'd ever seen—lots of fresh fruits and baked breads. There was even a guy standing by a skillet waiting to make you an omelet with whatever fixin's you wanted. And man could Pooh put it down. He must have went through the line about ten times and nobody said nothing. I went through it twice myself. I didn't know when we might eat again since neither of us had any more money.

We ate and didn't say a word to each other until after we checked out and were standing out front of the hotel. Pooh looked at me and said, "Are you angry with me?"

"No sir, I'm not, but don't be prying into my personal business. What happened between me and my son is our business and not anybody else's. So I'd appreciate it if you would keep your nose where it belongs. Now how do you suggest we get to Tuscumbia from here?"

Pooh thought a minute and held up his thumb.

# Chapter 10

I was still a little irritated. "What the hell does a thumb up mean?"

Then he turned it sideways in the universal sign of hitchhiking.

"You got to be kiddin' me! We're going to hitchhike? Do you really think that's the way to go?" I didn't want to say it, but what I was thinking was most people don't pick up hitchhikers much anymore, and no one was gonna put his big butt in their car, but I didn't want to hurt his feelings.

"Trust me. We'll get a ride. So let's go out there by the road. You'll see."

Now you're not going to believe this, but we stood there less than two minutes and the first car that came along stopped, pulled over, and the man waved for us to come get in.

"Good morning. Where you fellas headed this fine morning?"

Pooh got in the backseat because I called shotgun first thing. "I reckon we're going to Tuscumbia," I said to the man. "My name is Billy Bob Coker, but you can call me Bubba and the fella sittin' in the back is Pu Tai, but you can call him Pooh. That's what I call him, to his face anyways."

"My name is Thomas Orr, but you can call me Tom. I live over in Sheffield and can take you that far and if you don't mind me stopping at the house for just a minute to run inside and tend to something then I'll take you to Tuscumbia."

Before I could say a word, Pooh said, "That would be fine with us. I would love to meet your friend." Shit, there he goes again, knowing things that he couldn't know.

"Then it's settled. We'll stop by the house and then head on over to Tuscumbia." Tom smiled and took a deep breath, the kind that relaxes you real good and he sort of looked at Pooh the way you do when you think you know someone there ain't no way in hell you could know.

We drove the six or seven miles and talked about the weather and Tom asked me where I was from and I told him. Of course, he knew several folks from the Scottsboro area and he had a cousin that lived there and he'd been to Unclaimed Baggage several times. Turns out he works at Browns Ferry nuclear power plant as a foreman. He's a big fella, not fat, just big-boned. He had a crew cut, a close-cropped beard that had lots of gray in it, and he had lots of freckles but mostly he just looked like a regular kind of guy.

We got to his house, a pretty nice-looking ranch house built in the sixties or seventies.

"You boys come on in. I'll just be a minute or two."

We sat down on the couch and he went down the hall I guessed to the bedroom to see his wife or something. He called out, "Would either of you care for a beer or a cola?"

Before we could answer we heard the bedroom door shut. I was hoping this would only take a minute or two like he said 'cause I was a little nervous being in someone's home I didn't know. Pooh looked like he'd been there all his life, so much so he got up and sat in the blue recliner and shut his eyes and did the finger-thumb thing while I paced around the room. I started looking around the room and saw pictures of Tom and what looked like a real good friend. The two guys in one photo had their arms around each other. I figured they were probably drunk when they took the picture, but then I saw one where Tom was sittin' in the other guy's lap. I figured they must have really been knocking quite a few beers back at the time that picture was taken. Everyone does stupid stuff when they're shitfaced. Hell, one time I even grabbed old Chigger by the neck, gave him a noogie, and told him how much I loved him. When he reminded me of it the next day, I said I didn't recall because I was too drunk, but it was a lie. Rednecks are allowed to say they love their kids, their dog, their truck, and sometimes their wife a few times each year, but it's good not to make a habit of that or they'll start wanting you and expecting you to say it all the time.

About this time, Tom came into the living room. "Boys, I'm not going to be able to take you to Tuscumbia after all. Something has come up and I'm going to need to stay here and take care of it."

Before Tom could finish what he was saying, Pooh said, "No problem. We have plenty of time. Besides, like I said in the car, I'd like very much to meet your friend and I know Bubba wants to."

Tom looked hesitantly at me. His eyes were lowered like he wasn't sure about something. "Is that true, Bubba?"

"Sure. Why not?"

"Well, he is pretty sick and while I get the sense Mr. Pooh here won't mind, I don't want to impose on you." His voice was a little shaky.

Pooh looked at me, "Come on in with me, Bubba. Trust me."

We walked in and I was shocked to see Tom's friend lying there. He was a slender, pasty man with neatly cropped brown hair and a broad forehead and a real narrow pointed chin. He didn't look none too good I can tell ya.

"Pooh, this is Billy Noble. Meet Pu Tai." Pooh leaned over and kissed Billy on both cheeks.

I stepped over to the bed and shook his hand, which wasn't much of a handshake. "Nice to meet you. So you are Tom's roommate? Looks like you're not quite up to snuff."

"No, I'm not Tom's roommate, I'm his partner. It's very nice to meet you. Sorry you have to see me this way. I wasn't expecting Tom to bring over company. We don't have much company these days," Billy spoke with a wheezy voice.

"What kind of business you fellas in?" I asked a little sheepishly. "I thought you worked for TVA, Tom."

"I do, but we're not business partners, we're life partners. We have been together for twelve years. We finally tied the knot in Massachusetts last year because it isn't legal here in Alabama." Tom was smiling before he realized what he'd said.

I started backing out of the room. "You mean you two are married to each other? Screw me, Pooh, I mean not screw me; shit I got to get out of here. Come on, Pooh, we can catch another ride to Tuscumbia." I headed out the door and walked outside. I could barely catch my breath. I didn't want to stand in the yard for fear someone might see me, but I didn't have any other place to go. I sure wasn't going back inside. I must have waited for about an hour before I realized Pooh wasn't coming out. I figured I'd have to go in and get him, but I sure didn't want to. I knocked on the door and Tom came and let me in and I scooted by him, turning my body sideways not wanting to get too close or anything.

"I'm sorry I said all of that in the bedroom Bubba, but Billy and I have decided we're not hiding our feelings for each other anymore. We just don't have the time for such bullshit. We love each other and that's all there is to it. So I'm sorry if you're uncomfortable with us but that's just the way it is. Your friend Pooh is still with Billy if you want to go talk to him." Tom was sounding more firm like in his voice and he was now looking me in the eye, but I kept lowering mine to the floor like he was earlier.

When I went into the bedroom I saw Pooh leaning over Billy from the right side of the bed that had them bars on it and they were down on that side. I'll never forget the expression on Pooh's face. It's the way I remember my ex-wife Shirley looking at our son right after he was born. I don't think I'd ever seen that look on any man's face that I'd ever known. It took me a minute or two before I realized what he was doing. Pooh was giving the man a sponge bath. Billy was naked all over and nothing much there but skin and bones. He looked like pictures I'd seen of hungry children in India or Africa. I couldn't believe it. I got more than an eyeful I reckon and put my hands over my eyes. I couldn't stand to see no more. I asked Pooh to come outside with me for a minute 'cause I was getting ready to leave.

Pooh said he would, just as soon as he got finished and put Billy in some clean pajamas.

Pooh came out in the front yard and looked like nothing had happened.

"What in the hell is going on? You don't know these guys and the sick one is in his birthday suit and you're bathing him."

"You're pretty upset aren't you, Bubba? What is it about Tom and Billy that scares you so much?" Pooh sat down on the grass and I kept standing.

"What they're doing is unnatural and an abomination to the Lord. Men aren't supposed to do that stuff. Everyone knows that except liberal Democrat types. They're doing what that piece of white trash Big Dick accused us of being. I mean, for God's sake, they are homos and I can't stay in the house with homos! We got to get going to Tuscumbia and do whatever the hell we're going to do there. Now let's go." I talked way faster than I usually do. I almost sounded like I was from up North, I was speaking so fast.

Pooh looked at me and then looked at the sky. "Let me tell you a story."

"Oh, God, Pooh, not another story."

"One time there was a monk who lived all by himself in the woods in a small hut. He was a holy man and never bothered anybody, never hurt anybody. In the same village there was a young boy and girl who were just children themselves about fifteen or sixteen years old. They made love and the girl became pregnant. Now she knew for a fact if her parents ever found out they would disown her forever and the boy would lose his inheritance from his wealthy family. So when the baby came, the girl said it was the monk's child and that he forced her to have sex with him. Well the local authorities could not prove he forced himself on her, but the girl's father took the baby to the monk and said, 'You raped my daughter and you will take care of the child. That is the least you can do.' The monk looked at the angry father and all he said was, 'Is that so.' The monk took the little baby into his hut and cared for it and loved it as if it were his very own child. Several months went by and the girl confessed to the father that it was not the monk's baby and she was never raped and it was the boy who was the father. Her father, still angry, went to the monk and said, 'We want the child back. We know the child is not yours.' The monk looked at the child and then the man and all he said as he handed the little baby over was, 'Is that so,' and he turned around and went back in the hut."

"Well, thanks, Pooh, that explains everything!" I said, throwing my hands in the air.

"People are free to think whatever they want to. No matter what they think about you, you just do the next right thing, with the right attitude and the right effort." Pooh paused and I jumped in.

"Well, that may be true where you come from," I pointed to the sky, "but down here in the Deep South them kind of boys get the shit stomped out of them real regular like and fellas like me who are friends with the likes of them get the shit stomped out of them as well. It's one thing to be friends with an Asian guy but being caught being friends with homos is another. Now we got to get the hell out of here is all I'm saying."

"Is that so?" Pooh said as he got up and turned around and went back into the house. I scratched my balls and looked up into the sky and said a little prayer for Billy and Tom, asking the Lord to forgive me for going into the den of iniquity. Then I took a deep breath and went back in.

# Chapter 11

Tom greeted me at the door and was pretty damned surprised that I came back. I looked at him and wondered how this regular-looking fella from Alabama became one of these guys. I mean he looked perfectly normal to me. "Look, Tom, I don't know how to be around you folks. I mean, I'll be honest with you. There ain't ever been no man that I have ever seen that made me want to give him a . . . you know. So I don't know what I'm doing here or what to do except Pooh says we're going to stay so I guess that settles it. You will still take us to Tuscumbia tomorrow, won't ya?"

Tom looked at me and said, "Bubba, if every heterosexual man spoke as straightforward and direct as you just did we wouldn't be nearly as scared as we are. At least I know where you stand. And you are standing in my home and you are welcome. And let me be as equally direct so as to put your mind at ease. Being gay is not contagious, so you don't have to worry about catching it. We won't attack you in the night and take advantage of you. I won't take you shopping or give you a makeover like those guys on *Queer Eye* nor will I ask you to help me redecorate the house nor take care of Billy. But just so you know, mine and Billy's relationship, just like anyone who is in a committed one, goes way beyond our cocks and more into caring for and about each other. We've been monogamous for twelve years now."

Before Tom could finish, I had to say, "Okay, I got it! TMI now: Too Much Information. Thank you kindly for the reassurance."

About that time there was a knock on the door and in walked this good-looking woman. She grabbed Tom around the neck and hugged him and kissed him on the mouth—just a peck, but still, how could she do that was what I asked myself, her knowing where his mouth had been and all.

She appeared to be a strong woman in her thirties, from sturdy stock. Her skin had a deep bronze color that comes from being outdoors a lot and not from a tanning booth or a bottle like a lot of the girls at home. There were crow's-feet around her eyes and streaks of gray in her auburn hair. Her arms looked like they could tote just about anything she wanted to, and her hair was long like I fancy it. She was big-boned like my momma, but not fat. I like a woman who is not puny or frail.

"Hi, sweetie," Tom said after the kiss and hug. "Thank you for coming over again to lend a hand." He looked over to me. "Let me introduce you to a fella who will be spending the night with us tonight. Grace, this is Billy Bob Coker, but you can call him Bubba."

I looked at Grace and felt the way Pooh seems to feel about everybody we've met so far—like I've known her before. "Nice to meet you, ma'am. I'm not gay or anything, I just wanted you to know." I couldn't believe I said such a dufus thing.

She wrinkled her nose and furrowed her brow like she was smelling milk that had gone bad. "Well, pleased to meet you, Mr. Coker. I'm not gay either and I didn't think you were, but now that we've got that out of the way, what brings you to Sheffield?"

"Well, I'm from Scottsboro . . ."

"Scottsboro. I have an uncle and aunt that live over in Woodville. I bet you know them—Havel and Bernice Chitwood."

"Coach Havel and Mrs. Bernice are your kin? I'll be damned.

Your uncle was my coach in junior high football and my civics teacher in the ninth grade, and your aunt worked with me at Unclaimed Baggage. She's been there ever since it opened, I reckon."

With her hand on her hip, Grace said, "I'll be damned. It's a small world."

"I'm traveling with a big Asian guy, and he ain't gay either, no disrespect intended, Tom. We're headed to Tuscumbia 'cause he wants to show me something there that's important. You'll meet him soon. He's in there with Tom's, uh, friend right now. His name is Pu Tai, but everyone calls him Pooh. You'll see. Anyway, it's nice to meet you."

I figured she right off thought, "What a redneck!" though she sure did smile at me as she said to Tom with a real toothy grin, "How's my brother today? Is he feeling any better? I'll go in say hello and then I'll fix you boys up some good southern cooking. How would you like that, Bubba?"

"That would be finer than frog hair split four ways, ma'am."

She turned and went down the hall. Billy was her brother. Man that was something. I wondered how she dealt with the fact that he was a homosexual. She didn't seem embarrassed or nothing like I would have been to tell someone I had one of them in my family. I mean we can't say a lot of good things about our family tree given it's only got the one or two branches, but as far as I know we never had one of them in our family. Closest thing we came to it was when my grandmother on my momma's side married Charley Culpepper about twenty years after granddaddy died, and he had a son Tracy, who if he wasn't gay, damn sure missed his calling 'cause he sure acted like it. I mean there was nobody any more fairylike than him when he talked and walked.

Tom went back in the bedroom, and I sat down on the couch and pondered the situation a little bit and looked around for something to read to pass the time while they all were doing whatever they were doing in the bedroom.

On a shelf under the coffee table was a book called, *Living And Dying With AIDS*. Holy shit, man, I threw that book down like it was a hot coal. Goddamn, I knew it. That's why Billy looked like death warmed over. He had AIDS! Now I don't mind telling you I was sweating and nervous as a whore at an outdoor tent church revival. I went and washed my hands in real hot soapy water two or three times and was real careful to turn off the faucet with my elbow. I didn't want to catch this, and what I really wanted was to get the hell out of there, and I didn't know how I was going to do it. Pooh walked into the kitchen where I was freaking out.

# Chapter 12

"Bubba, you can't catch AIDS from touching things. Try to relax and trust me. Everything is going to be fine. We'll stay here tonight and go to Tuscumbia tomorrow."

Tom came out of the bedroom. "He's asleep now. Let's go out in the back and I'll show you fellas to the guesthouse Billy and I built a few years ago. I think you'll find it real comfortable."

I breathed a little sigh of relief because we weren't going to have to stay in the same house. The house was about nine hundred square feet with a huge ceiling and lots of windows and real rustic, just the kind of place I'd build for myself if I ever had the time and money. It had one couch that was a sleeper sofa and one of them Oriental couches; I told Pooh he could sleep on the pooh-ton.

Pooh lay down and closed his eyes. "So what do you think about Grace? She is very striking, isn't she?"

It was like he was reading my mind.

"You are attracted to her if I am correct. Why don't you go inside and see if you can help her with dinner and I'll meditate."

I decided I'd go in but wasn't about to offer to help with dinner. She might think I was like her brother and Tom after all. Generally, southern men don't cook or clean unless they just have to for themselves and only then until they find a good woman. I never once saw my daddy cook anything for us at home even when Momma was sick. He'd ask one of her sisters or his to come over and cook.

I went into the house and stood in the doorway for a minute or two watching her wash the vegetables in the sink, looking out the window, and singing an old Appalachian song I hadn't heard since my great grandmother died years ago.

"Oh, death, oh, death, how can it be. I am bound for eternity . . ."

She was singing it just like I remember great granny, shrill and high-pitched, and scary as hell but at the same time real soothing. I listened and I knew Tom and Billy could hear it as well and wondered what they thought about her singing such a song. Then it struck me. They all knew that he was gonna die real soon.

She quit singing after a while, and she turned around and saw me standing in the doorway. "I'm sorry. I didn't know you were there," she said as she cut up the okra and put the corn in the pot to boil.

"Where did you learn that song you were singing just now?" I asked.

"My grandmother taught it to me when I was a little girl. She was born up in the mountains near Asheville, North Carolina, and we'd go spend the summers with her. She didn't have any electricity, or indoor plumbing, but she knew all about plants, herbs, and all the old songs like that one. She also taught me everything I know about beekeeping. She made the best honey in the world and would go to town on trade day and sell it to buy the few things she didn't make or couldn't grow."

"Is that what you do for a living? beekeeping? I don't mean to pry into your personal business or anything. I'm just curious is all."

"Well, you know what they say, 'Curiosity killed the cat,'" she laughed.

"Yeah, and satisfaction brought him back."

"Yep, I'm a beekeeper, among other things. I'm also a massage therapist, and volunteer at the Wiregrass Hospice in Florence."

"You work in a massage parlor?"

"No. I'm a licensed massage therapist. There's never anything sexual about what I do, so don't get any wrong notions about me from the get go. I'm going to get up real early in the morning and tend to my bees. You ever seen bee colonies before?"

"Not up close."

"You are welcome to come along if you get up with the chickens."

"So yeah, let's go."

I helped her set the table and Tom and Pooh came in later and we had a real good supper. Before we started eating, Tom said, "Lord, we want to thank you for the food we are about to receive and for Bubba and Pooh being here with us. We ask you to forgive us of our sins and to be with my sweet Billy and make him as comfortable as possible. In Jesus' name, Amen."

Now I got to tell you that threw me for a loop. Here was this man who, you know, well, is a homosexual person who has to know he's sinning like hell, and here he is praying up a storm just like anybody. It just didn't make sense, but I didn't say anything. I just ate Grace's fried chicken, which was almost as good as my momma's, but her fried apple pies were the best things I'd had in my mouth in a long time. At the table there wasn't much talk. We were all pretty quiet, I reckon. It was mostly chit-chat, and then right before we got up Tom took a knife and clicked it against his tea glass.

"I'd like to make a toast to our guests. Thank them for being here with us. And to Grace, the best sister-in-law a man could ever have."

I stayed around to help Grace clean up a little. I picked up the plates and put the scraps in the garbage, but I didn't wash any dishes or dry them or anything like that. We talked a little about this and that and the other, and then I told her I was tired and needed to go to bed, and she gave me another invitation to join her the next morning and again I told her I would.

When I got to the guesthouse I overheard Pooh talking to somebody or himself, but I caught him as he was finishing the conversation, "I know, I know. I don't have much time left and I'm prepared to accept the consequences if your desired outcome is not achieved. Thank you, Namaste, Asalam, Alakam, Shalom, Shanti, Yohey, Amen." I figured he was talking to the Wise Ones though I didn't know what any of those words meant except "Amen" and "Thank you." It made me a little nervous.

"So, Bubba, you're going with Grace in the morning to see her bees?" He smiled.

"When you know shit before I tell you, it rattles me still. I don't know if I'm ever going to get used to it."

Pooh shrugged.

"Yes, I'm going with her. It's no big deal."

I took off my clothes and got into bed. "Pooh, how long are we really going to stay here with these folks? I mean, we are leaving tomorrow, aren't we?"

"I don't know just yet. Trust me; we'll know when it's time to leave. In the meantime, let's get some sleep and see what the morning brings."

Well, it took me a long time before I got to sleep. I just wasn't used to all this stuff and didn't know what to make of it. I did know there was something about Grace that sure as hell felt familiar and that I was looking forward to going to see her bees in the morning.

When I woke up I was thankful I didn't dream or if I did that I didn't remember them. I could smell bacon cooking from the main house and got up and fixed me some coffee and put on some hot water for Pooh's green tea the boys had on a shelf. I took my coffee and went to the main house to see what was going on and help Grace with setting the table for breakfast. Pooh was still sound asleep, and when I got to the house, Grace said it would just be the two of us. Tom and Billy would be sleeping late 'cause Tom was up all night with Billy, who wasn't doing so good. We ate our breakfast quietly so as not to wake them up, and she wrapped everything up in tinfoil and we headed off to see her bees. We got in her VW van and headed for Hawk Pride Mountain, which is at just about the farthest end of the Appalachian chain and about fifteen or so miles from Sheffield.

# Chapter 13

The fog held tightly to the mountain. The rolling hills reminded me a lot of Scottsboro. I started feeling a little homesick. As we drove I remembered the time my momma and daddy sent me to my granddaddy's when we were still living in Detroit. My daddy and momma and several of my aunts and uncles joined the hillbilly migration up there right after the war to work in the automobile factories. We lived up there until I was nine.

One time they sent me to Alabama on a Greyhound bus when I was six years old. It took about twenty-four hours to make the trip and I was scared shitless. I must have talked to the bus driver all the way down there when I wasn't asleep. I remember him being a real nice fella, for a Yankee. When I got to my granddaddy's I remember getting a letter from my mom a day or two later and going out underneath a pecan tree and reading it and crying, I was so homesick. I guess in a way I've always been sort of homesick even when I am home, which doesn't make a lick of sense. I told Grace about this and while I was pretty sad, she was even sadder. I looked over at her just as we were pulling into the pasture where she kept her bees and she had tears in her eyes and she said, "I'm so sorry that happened to you. You must have been scared to death to be all alone for so long. What were your parents thinking to send a little boy on a trip like that?"

"It wasn't that bad. I was always old for my age in some ways," was all I knew to say.

"I'd never send a six-year-old off by himself no matter how old he acted. You were just a little boy. Do you have children?"

Before I could answer, she said, "I bet you don't or you'd know how wrong they were to do that."

"I never sent my son away like that, but if I were to be real honest with you I'd have to say I walked away from him when he was about the age I was when they sent me south. But I'd rather not talk about that if it's all right with you. Let's see them bees." I was glad she didn't push me to talk about me or my boy.

She looked at me with heaviness or sadness or something that I wasn't used to seeing. We walked out into the field and there were all these huge oak trees and some of the bees were in the field and some under trees. Grace's face lit up like a Christmas tree the closer we got to them.

"Did you know if we didn't have bees we wouldn't have pumpkins, apples, onions, and lots of other things we eat every day? One-third of all the food we eat comes from being pollinated by honeybees. The bee only lives for six weeks, and in that entire little life she'll make about one-half a teaspoon of honey. The male's only job is to mate with the queen and then die."

She went on and on with real interesting stuff on bees. I worried she'd die from not taking a breath. I might have to perform CPR, and I didn't know how but it did involve mouth to mouth, and I already had figured I'd like to try that the first time I saw her.

She finally paused and started putting smoke on the bees—to calm them down, she said. "Bee venom is used to relieve pain like arthritis and migraines. Alexander the Great, Confucius, and others used bee-sting therapy. There is this ancient rock painting in one of those old caves—I saw a picture of it once—from six thousand B.C. where people were robbing beehives. Did you know there were no bees at all in America until Plymouth Rock and that the Indians called them the white man's mosquitoes? I'm sorry—when I get a little nervous I tend to make lists of things to try to calm myself down."

"Damn woman, you know your bee history, don't you?" I smiled at her and she smiled back.

"Sorry about that. I get a little carried away when I start talking about these marvelous little creatures, don't I?"

"Don't you get stung a lot working with them?"

"Not very often. Tell the truth, I'd rather be stung by them than bitten by a mosquito."

She worked with her hives scraping honey into a bucket. I sat underneath a tree and just watched her. She told me later that bees communicate with each other by dancing, and that's what she looked like as she was working her hives, more like a dancer and a graceful one at that. Finally, after she finished she caught a few and put them in a jar. She said she was gonna take them back home and let Billy get stung a few times 'cause it seemed to help lessen his pain.

"Can I ask you about Billy, if you don't mind?" I was a little nervous to ask, I don't mind telling you. "What do you think about him being . . . you know?" I wobbled my hand 'cause I didn't want to say the word.

"Oh, you mean gay?" she said quickly.

"Yeah, gay."

"It's not the life I would wish on anyone, especially my brother, especially down here in the South, but anywhere for that matter. It's a hard, dangerous way to live, but it's not for me to judge. I love him. I support him. I care for him and I just always wanted him to be happy." She paused and took a deep breath and a tear ran down her cheek.

"Well, like it says in the Bible, 'Judge not lest ye be not judged.'"

Grace frowned and blinked at me. "Uh, yeah, something like that. He's my brother and he loves Tom. I was so glad when he finally found someone as good as Tom is to him. You should have seen their wedding. I wish Mom and Dad could have gone. They both were beautiful in their tuxes."

"Are your mom and dad dead?" I asked.

"No, they are still alive, but they pretty much disowned Billy when he was in college because that's when he came out of the closet and announced it to us. They don't call or come around much since he's been sick. Listen; let's change the subject. I know it's kind of early yet, but normally after I take care of my bees I go for a swim over at Buzzard's Roost. It's not far from here. You up for a cold dip in a creek?"

"I didn't bring a bathing suit."

"Neither did I." Her face glowed. "Let's go."

# Chapter 14

We got in the van and talked all the way to the creek about all kinds of things. If this were a movie I'd be hearing Donovan singing "Wear Your Love Like Heaven" as we drove through the country looking at trees and playing I Spy and real romantic stuff like that. As soon as we got to the creek, she parked the van and started running toward the water. At the same time she was taking off her shirt, shorts, and under things, throwing them down on the ground. I wish it were a movie 'cause this part would be in slow motion. Since it was real life it went way too fast and I barely could see anything, but what I saw I sure did like.

She jumped in the water and I stood on the bank and watched her splash around and dive under. "Come on in. It's not that cold," she said.

"I'm really not a very good swimmer. You have fun and I'll just sit here and enjoy the scenery." Really I just didn't want her to see me naked in broad daylight and the truth is I'm not exactly hung like a horse, and if I jumped in the cold water my dick would shrink almost out of sight and that wouldn't be something I'd care for her to see.

"Cluck, cluck, cluck, cluck. Somebody is a big old chicken." She was laughing and she had gotten close enough for me to see her real good like and splashing, so, hell, I dove in with all my clothes on and dunked her a couple of times. "Who you calling chicken?"

We swam around for about ten or fifteen minutes, and I was freezing my ass and my little dick off, but I didn't want her to know it. She wrapped her legs around my waist as I swung her around and around. I loved seeing Grace naked and having so much fun. We finally got out and sat on some rocks and I was shivering so hard my teeth were rattling. "I'll run to the van and get some towels and blankets. When I get back you get out of those wet clothes and get yourself warm," she yelled.

She returned with a towel, beach blanket, a pair of shorts, some sweatpants, and a couple of T-shirts. "Here, I think you can fit into these. Tom left them in the van the last time we all went swimming. Damn, that's been nearly a year ago now before Billy got so sick."

I swear she took off the beach towel she had wrapped around her right there and started putting on the dry clothes. I turned my back to her 'cause my privates were still looking pretty puny. I guessed that we wouldn't be doing the wild thing since she got dressed and all. I was kinda glad 'cause there was something about her that made me want to know her first before we had sex, which was something I'd never really felt before. Now I've never really been good at talking much, but for some reason I can't explain that's what I wanted to do. I wanted to know more about her.

"So tell me, Grace, I know why you started keeping bees but what about being a massage therapist? When did that and the hospice thing, and what exactly is that, come about?"

"Well, my first real boyfriend got hurt in a car accident when we were in college, and I would give him a massage almost every night before going to bed. I could see how much it helped and I figured if I really knew how to do it right it would really make a difference. I took these night classes and got into it so much that I went ahead and got my license. After I graduated I was a waitress for a while, then I tried my hand at photography and some other odds and ends, and when I was about thirty I decided to go full-time and opened a massage therapy office and been doing it ever since." She paused and dried her hair with the towel. When the sun hit it just right, you could see streaks of red.

"Don't you get a lot of freaks who think you are going to have sex with them?" I asked.

"I did at first. But I can pretty much tell who these guys are over the phone, and I don't make an appointment with them."

"As for hospice I started volunteering when Billy took ill as a way to build up some good karma for his and my sake."

"What's karma?" I was curious 'cause I'd heard the word before when Pooh was talking to Captain Sam.

"I'm sure you heard the old saying, 'What goes around comes around.'"

I nodded.

"Karma is the belief that what we do or don't do counts and determines how we live the next life."

Before she could finish the sentence, I asked, "So you believe we are coming back? Us Christians don't believe that. Are you a Buddhist or something?"

"No, I'm not a Buddhist, though I did study it some in college and have read some books on it and other religions. Does the thought of coming back upset you?"

I really didn't know what to say. My granddaddy always said, "Never discuss politics and religion" and here we were knee-deep in one of them already. "Well, let's put it this way. I'm what you call a backsliding Christian." I turned around and pointed to my back. "See all those skid marks from drinking, drugging a little, gambling, screwing?" She started laughing and so did I.

"Is Pooh a Buddhist?" she seemed real serious like.

"I reckon. He sure doesn't talk like no Christian. He meditates and he knows all kinds of stuff before it happens, and he seems to care for your brother in a way you don't see people going to church regular doing, except maybe for that Mother Teresa woman. Truth is, I still don't know much about him." Right then I realized I knew more about this woman I was talking to than I did about Pooh.

# Chapter 15

"I think it's time we get back. I need to fix lunch for Tom and help feed Billy. Thank you for coming with me this morning. You've been great company. I'm sorry you have to leave today."

She looked kinda sorrowful and I felt kinda sad, which is unusual for me. My ex used to say I wouldn't know a feeling if it bit me on the ass.

On the way back to the house we stopped and got some groceries at Foodland and then some gas, so we didn't have much time to talk. When we walked into Tom and Billy's house we could hear Pooh talking to Billy in the bedroom.

Grace said, "I'm going to check on my brother. Would you mind taking in the groceries and starting lunch? I'll be in to help in just a minute." She headed down the hall before I could tell her I don't cook.

I looked at the kitchen. Now talk about a bull in a china shop. I knew I'd probably break shit, and the main thing I'd break is the redneck code of conduct that clearly states that the kitchen is a woman's place and that only pussy-whipped men, traitors to their sex, are ever caught doing woman's work. Everything else was changing—here I was traveling with my hallucination that everybody else could see, working on a towboat after saying I never would again, practically living with gay guys, and wanting to talk with a woman more than I wanted to screw her. I was going to lose my membership in good ol' boys society if I didn't watch out. Oh, hell, I'd already lost it, and my mind.

The only problem now was what to fix. She had a chicken and vegetables, but I sure as shit didn't know how to cook it. So I cracked some eggs in a bowl and even picked out the shells and beat the hell out of them with a fork like I'd seen cooks in the Waffle House do, pulled the bacon apart and stuck it in the frying pan and popped some bread in the toaster. They were just going to have to eat breakfast again 'cause that's the best I could do, and I got it all done before Grace got into the kitchen. I only broke two dishes in the process. In less than thirty minutes I'd turned into a regular chef Boyardee.

"Look at you, Bubba! You don't need my help." She just stared at the eggs and then over at the broken dishes and said, "I love breakfast anytime of the day and I know the others will too. I'll set the table and then take something in for Billy or would you like to do the honors?"

"You mean feed your brother?" Before she could answer, Pooh came into the kitchen. "I think that would be a wonderful gesture of thanks for their hospitality," he said, and I could tell he was serious.

"But, but, what if . . . you know, what if . . . oh, fuck a duck in a truck. Yeah, I'll feed him." Pooh and Grace looked at each other and smiled. "You two eat your breakfast and keep mine warm I reckon. But if either of you tell anyone about this I'll deny it to my grave."

About that time Tom was coming down the hall in his underwear. "Good morning, Bubba, how did you like Grace's bees? And for that matter, how do you like Grace? She's a sweetie, isn't she?"

"Loved the bees, Grace is great. I made some lunch, but it's breakfast again and now I'm going to take this food into your husband or wife or whatever you call him and if anybody else asks me to do another unnatural thing this morning, I don't know what I'll do!"

"Okay. I hear you, Bubba. Thank you. I'm going to eat and then I got to get to work. Will I see you and Pooh this evening when I get home?"

"I doubt it, but then what the hell do I know? You'll have to ask him." Again I scooted past him in the hall and stood at the door for a minute and then I walked in. The tray was shaking a little.

As soon as Billy saw it was me, he looked up and smiled. "So who wants to go first, should I blow you or you blow me?"

I felt all the blood drain from my head.

Billy laughed and then started losing his breath. "I'm sorry," he said. "I was just pulling your leg. Tom and Pooh told me you are a little anxious to be here. I just wanted to reduce the tension."

"That's all right. I knew you were kidding." I didn't, but I didn't want him to know that. "How are you feeling today?" I put the tray on the stand by his bed.

"Not too good. I can feed myself, but I'd appreciate the company while I eat, if you don't mind."

Billy talked much more proper like than Tom or me. I found out later he used to be a professor of English at the university over in Florence.

"So . . . Bubba, is it? What brings you to this part of God's country?" He asked in between dropping scrambled eggs on his pajamas.

"Here, let me help you with that. I don't mind. Just don't try no funny stuff."

That made Billy laugh some, but he coughed for a while after.

"Bubba, I haven't been able to try any funny stuff for a while now, so you don't have to worry. Could you put a straw in my water and give me a sip?"

"Sure can. To answer your question, I'm just along for the ride with Pooh, and I have no idea what I'm doing here."

"Can I ask you a question?" I asked, though I couldn't look him in the eye. I just stared at his mouth as I put the food slowly in.

"Sure. As long as it isn't about me being gay."

"No. It ain't that. It's about Grace."

"The sweetest sister in the whole world. What do you want to know?"

"Is she spoken for?"

"Do you mean is she seriously involved with anyone? The answer is no and hasn't been for quite some time. She stays pretty busy with her bees, her massage practice, and taking care of me and Tom. Are you interested?"

"No, no, nothing like that. I was just curious as all get out. I figured someone as beautiful and as nice as she is was at least being courted by someone from around here is all. She's a pretty thing; I'll say that for her and real smart, too. I'd bet a dollar to a donut she's more interested in educated fellas than an old country boy like me."

"Don't be so sure. We come from the same part of the country as you do. She probably told you about our great grandmother who lived in the mountains near Asheville, and our father's people came from over near Pigeon Forge, Tennessee. So while both of us went to college we're still hillbillies at heart."

I finished feeding him and he looked awful tired, so I figured he needed his rest and all, so I gathered up the stuff and went into the kitchen to eat and I overheard Pooh telling Grace that we would be staying two or three more days, that he had at least that amount of time we could spare.

"We're staying two more days?" I said as I put the dishes in the sink.

"Yes. I am running out of time, but Billy asked me and you to do something for him because Tom and Grace can't do it alone."

Before he could finish I jumped in, "Do what? I thought we were leaving today?" I acted madder than I really was because deep down inside I wanted to get to spend a little more time with Grace and I was still worried a little about being in the same house with two gay guys, but that was beginning to settle down.

"Billy said to me this morning that normally every spring since they've lived here together that he has put in a garden and that he wanted to see one more garden planted, and I told him we would at least get it started. The only problem is that the last time I had a garden—" Pooh looked over at Grace, who was sort of looking pleased with the news, I reckon. "Well, let's just say it's been a long time, so you are going to have to teach me. I know you know about gardens."

"I guess." I pointed up, "They told you that as well?"

"No, they didn't have to. You told me that a redneck knows how to plant a garden. Right?"

"Well, yeah, I know enough to get by. But that will be a full two days' work, so I reckon we'd better get our asses in gear if we're going to ever get out of here, no disrespect intended, Grace."

"None taken," Grace said. "I'll help as much as I can."

"Ah, then it is settled," Pooh said. "We'll begin the garden tomorrow, but this afternoon we're going to Tuscumbia."

# Chapter 16

Me, Grace, and Pooh climbed in her van. Pooh pretty much filled up the back and I rode shotgun.

Grace looked at her rear-view mirror. "Pooh, where in Tuscumbia do you want to go?"

"Yeah, exactly what's in Tuscumbia you want me to see?" I asked.

"Helen Keller's birthplace: Ivy Green. We're going to take a tour of the home of a great humanitarian and teacher. Mark Twain said that Helen Keller was a fellow Caesar, Alexander, Napoleon, Shakespeare, and the rest of the immortals and that she would be as famous in a thousand years as she was in his day. And Twain was right—I knew them all."

I looked at Pooh and then at Grace and swallowed real hard. "He means he has read and studied them all, right Pooh? That's what you meant." I wasn't sure Grace was ready to hear the truth about Pooh just yet.

I don't think she heard him anyway, because she was paying attention to her driving. There had formed a goober chain in front of her, which is a long line of bad, country drivers doing twenty miles an hour in a thirty-five zone, who come into town once a month whether they need to or not and then they act like they've never been to town before.

"I know who Helen Keller is, sort of, well I mean kind of. She was blind. When we were kids, if somebody tripped over something or garbled up a word or something we'd call them Helen. I feel kinda bad now that I'm saying it." I looked at Grace hoping she wasn't too offended by my callousness.

"I've been here a couple of times," said Grace. "And I've seen the movie *The Miracle Worker*, with Ann Bancroft and Patty Duke. It was intense. But I can always see her home again; it's beautiful."

About that time we pulled into Ivy Green and there was a sign on the gates that said, CLOSED FOR RENOVATIONS.

Grace sighed. "Sorry about that, Pooh. Looks like we won't be able to see it after all." She put the van in reverse and started backing out.

"Sure we will," Pooh said cheerfully. "Trust me, you two."

Just as he said this a woman came walking out to the gate. She was an odd-looking woman in her sixties or seventies. She had long silver hair, which looked kind of hippielike, and she wore a long black skirt and a white shirt kinda like the kind you wear with a tuxedo. A cameo brooch was attached to the shirt and she wore old-fashioned dark glasses. She looked real neat. She opened the gate and motioned for us to come on in. Grace looked at me and I looked at Pooh, who was smiling ear-to-ear. She slid the car into the parking space.

The strange woman met Pooh on the sliding door side, and they hugged and he kissed her on both cheeks and she kissed him.

"I am so glad you could come. I was afraid I wasn't going to see you. I expected you yesterday. But never mind. I'm just glad you are here. These are your friends, I take it. And you young man," she held her hand out for me to take, "You and this young woman must be good people to be traveling with this fine man."

"May I introduce you to my friends, Miss S? This is my traveling companion, Billy Bob Coker, and this young woman is Grace Noble. Bubba and Grace, this is my dear friend, Miss S."

Well, Grace looked at me and then at Pooh and then at Miss S. "May I ask what the S stands for?" Grace said.

"Would you folks like a cup of tea before I give you the tour of this lovely house and grounds?" She seemed to not hear Grace's question.

Just as Miss S was headed into the kitchen, Grace said again, "May I ask you your last name? In a small town like this and Sheffield where I live everybody knows everybody."

Again she seemed to not hear the question. "Would anyone care for some cake?" Miss S asked and then disappeared into the kitchen.

"She must not have heard you," Pooh said to Grace. "I'm sure she's not being impolite. I think I'll go help with the tea," and he disappeared into the kitchen as well.

We were seated in the parlor and Miss S brought the silver serving tray with a silver teapot and poured us all tea and cut each of us a piece of cake.

"Helen's mother was a tall, statuesque blonde with blue eyes and she was twenty years younger than her husband, Captain Keller, a loyal Southerner who proudly served in the Confederate Army during the Civil War. This house they lived in looks like it did then, just simple, white clapboard, built in 1820 by Helen's grandparents. When Helen was nineteen months old, she fell terribly ill. The doctors called it 'brain fever.' Most modern doctors think it was probably scarlet fever." Miss S paused and looked real sad. "Pardon me for losing my composure. Anyway she was expected to die. Her illness left her deaf and blind. Did you know that it was Alexander Graham Bell, the inventor of the telephone, who came up with the sign language that allowed Helen to communicate? After we have our tea we shall go out to the pump."

"Isn't that where Miss Helen said her first word—water?" I asked mostly to show off a little.

"Let me summarize and say Miss Helen, with all the barriers placed in front of her, overcame them, perhaps because being blind she just couldn't see them. She was the first deaf, blind person to earn a bachelor of arts degree and went on to tour the world and became an inspiration to many, many people. Do you see, Bubba, what I'm saying?"

I looked at her and scratched my head.

We then followed Miss S to the little cottage, in back of the main house, where Anne and Helen lived together. We found out that Helen Keller died on June 1, 1968, and her ashes were deposited next to her teacher Anne Sullivan. I still had no idea why Pooh wanted us to visit this place. I know I'm not the sharpest knife in the drawer, but I knew Pooh was up to something. We sat down in the cottage and Miss S started talking again about Helen Keller and how important she was and that how if she were born today her life would have been completely different. Anne said Helen's lifelong dream was to be able to talk, something that she never could do."

I asked Miss S, the tour guide, how Miss Keller could do all the things she did? Miss S spoke slowly and clearly. I'll never forget what she said.

Miss S stared at the sky, like I'd seen Pooh do several times on this trip, and finally after a few moments of silence she said, "Helen said, 'Although the world is full of suffering, it is full also of the overcoming of it. . . . Everything has its wonders, even darkness and silence, and I learn whatever state I am in, therein, to be content."

Then Miss S looked straight at me as though she was seeing right through me. "Bubba, Helen also said somewhere that, 'Life is either a daring adventure or nothing. Security does not exist in nature, nor do the children of men as a whole experience it. Avoiding danger is no safer in the long run than exposure. . . . I seldom think of my limitations.'"

I think, but I'm not sure, she was saying the fact that I'm a hillbilly with only a twelfth-grade education, that I shouldn't let that be what puts the brakes on me learning new ways of seeing things.

"You have eyes, and Helen was always fond of saying, 'It's a terrible thing to see and have no vision.' Do you have vision, son?" Miss S asked politely.

I thought real hard for a minute and looked at Pooh and then Grace and finally, said, "Yes ma'am, 20/20?" They all laughed. I wasn't real sure why, but I laughed along with them.

"I'm sure you're tired of hearing the ramblings of an old half-blind woman. Pooh, I know you only have so much time left so good-bye, dear friend, and bye to you Grace. Bubba, take care of each other."

We waved good-bye and walked toward the van. Grace and I both turned around at the same time to wave a final good-bye to Miss S, but when we did, she was gone.

# Chapter 17

We drove back to the house in complete silence. Pooh sat in the back with his fingers and thumbs together and his eyes closed. Maybe Grace was thinking what I was thinking: that there was something mighty strange going on at Ivy Green.

When we arrived, Pooh went to the guest house and Grace checked in on Billy, who was sound asleep. She came back into the living room. "Would you like a beer, or a Coke, or anything?"

"I'll take a beer," I said.

She brought it to me and we sat down on the couch and just looked at each other. Finally, she broke the silence. "Who do you think we met at Ivy Green, and who do you think Pooh really is?"

"I'm not real sure. Sometimes I think everything that has happened to me since the first time I met Pooh is just a dream or a nightmare that just keeps going on and on, or at least that is until I met you. Now no matter what happens I don't think of it as a nightmare, although it just gets weirder and weirder. I thought it would never get any weirder than what happened to Uncle Ethridge, on my momma's side. Everyone calls him Booger, I'm not real sure why, but back in 1989 he and a bunch of others in the town of Fyffe, which is real close to Scottsboro, reported seeing a banana-shaped bright light and crops pushed down in circles, and he and some other fella's cattle was mutilated. It looked like someone had used surgical instruments to make the cuts. This led to the police over there reporting they saw a triangular object that passed over their heads and didn't make a sound. Fyffe was designated as the official UFO capital of Alabama, and to this day every August they hold a UFO festival and it's one wacko, weirdo weekend. Chigger and I went last year just to see all the loonies. So after that, hell I don't know what to think anymore.

Grace laughed.

"Who do you think it was at Helen Keller's house?" I asked her.

Grace took a couple of sips of her beer before answering, "I'm not sure, but it is kind of spooky the way the gate had a closed sign on it and she sort of just appeared."

I added, "How her last name began with an *s* like Helen Keller's teacher, Anne Sullivan. And what about the way she was dressed? Plus, how she seemed to know Pooh. Then, poof, she was gone. I don't know what's happening." I figured it was time. "Speaking of poof . . . you want to know who Pooh is?"

"Yes, I do."

"He poofed right into my life and I'm afraid if I tell you the whole story you'll poof right out of mine, because you'll think I'm totally insane, but here she goes."

I told her about the suitcase and the music and the green colored lights and how he kept saying "trust me." We talked about Captain Sam and how he knew Pooh, and I told her stuff he said to me and about the conversations with ole Jim. I even told Grace about the fight. When I got through, I was surprised she hadn't left and called the guys with white coats and butterfly nets.

"I believe you. Why would you lie? The truth is, I have never believed in coincidences. There is something very strange about all of these chance meetings. I remember something Helen Keller said that I learned in school, 'The best and most beautiful things in the world cannot be seen or even touched—they must be felt with the heart.' She was right and I feel in my heart that something special is supposed to happen if we allow it to."

"What do you think is supposed to happen?" I asked sort of reluctantly, a little fearful of the answer.

"I don't know and I don't know much about mystical things, but I do believe in miracles. Right now I feel we need to focus on the here-and-now, and we don't have much time to put in the garden before you and Pooh have to leave. We better go to Cold Water Feed and Seed Store and get what we need."

# Chapter 18

Tuscumbia is a sweet town thanks to Harvey Robbins of Robbins Tire and Rubber. He poured his own money into beautifying the place by planting colorful little pansies on every corner and adding cobblestone walkways to the downtown area, and the park downtown is something to behold.

At Cold Water we bought squash, corn, eggplant, and green bean seeds, along with some fertilizer and some sunflower seeds to help keep the bugs off. For the first time on the trip, I felt really at home and like I knew what I was doing. I remembered, before my dad and mom split the quilts with a "see ya'll," he would tell me I was dumb and retarded every time he would try to show me how to do something. That stuck to me like a wad of gum on the bottom of my shoe. But one thing I knew, thanks to my granddaddy on his side, was how to plant and tend to a garden. In junior high, I belonged to the 4-H Club and Future Farmers of America. I took first prizes for my tomatoes and squash for being the biggest and best color two years in a row. I also took first prize in the ninth grade in hog raising. Miss Piggy weighed in right at four hundred and fifty pounds. I loved that pig. I sure did hate to eat her.

When we got back to the house, it was pretty late and about time for supper. Tom wouldn't be home for another couple of hours. Pooh was in the bedroom with Billy. Grace and I went in to say hello, and Pooh was just finishing up reading from the book he held in his hands. Together we listened to the last few passages.

Billy smiled and had a real peaceful look on his face. "Pooh, would you mind reading the last four or five things the Dalai Lama said. I'd like Grace and Bubba to hear them."

Pooh said, "Sure, I'd be glad to. I could use hearing them myself again. 'Follow the three R's: respect for self, respect for others, and responsibility for all your actions. When you lose, don't lose the lesson. When you realize you've made a mistake, take immediate steps to correct it. A loving atmosphere in your home is the foundation for your life.'"

By the time Pooh read the last one Billy was asleep. "Pooh, who said those things you were reading?" I asked.

Pooh looked surprised, "Oh, that was the Dalai Lama."

"What is a Dalai Lama?"

"The Dalai Lama is a holy man from Tibet. He is the world's most famous Buddhist other than Richard Gere," answered Grace. "Thank you Pooh for reading to my brother and all the compassion and concern you have shown him these last couple of days. I'm going to fix you fellas and Tom some supper. Tomorrow we'll get up real early and start that garden we promised to put in for my brother."

We ate some country-fried steak with mashed potatoes and gravy, and Grace made some damn good biscuits. I helped her with the dishes—this time I washed and she dried—and then I went to the guest cottage and caught the tail end of one of my all-time favorite movies, *Field of Dreams*, on the TV. Pooh watched it with me and said he'd known all the ball players personally, and he especially enjoyed meeting Burt Lancaster and did a pretty poor imitation of him.

We turned off the television and Pooh got real serious like. "Bubba, I don't have much time left on this trip. We have to leave for the final leg of it day after tomorrow, and if I don't succeed in the mission the Wise Ones gave me the consequences for us both . . ." He paused and looked a little sad. "Let's just say they are less than optimal."

I didn't know what the last word meant, but I guessed he was trying to say we needed to get our asses in gear, get the lead out, put the pedal to the metal; you know those kinds of things. "What do you mean by 'consequences'?"

"We'll discuss it first thing in the morning. Now to sleep, perchance to dream," he said, and then there was silence. Pooh was sound asleep. And damn if I didn't have another dream.

In this dream Billy and I were planting a garden, and then Dolly Parton came walking into the garden leading a llama behind her and talking to the seeds and every time she said something the seeds would instantly become tomatoes or a squash and then she looked at us and said to me, "I am the Dolly and this is the llama." Then Dolly looked at Billy and took his hands. "These words I give you Billy are from his Holiness, 'It never occurs to us that we will die.'" As soon as she said it, Billy died and a big yellow sunflower sprung up from where he was standing. Dolly looked at me and said, "If you see the Buddha on the road, you must kill him. You should continue doing this until you receive a clear indication, for example in your dreams, that your unwholesome deeds have been purified.'"

I shot up out of bed and looked around the room. It felt so real. Stumbling around in the dark, I woke up Pooh.

"Bubba, are you all right? Did you have another dream?"

"I guess, but it sure seemed real. It was like it really happened, and it scared the crap out of me, I don't mind telling you." I was a little out of breath.

"Sit down. Take a deep breath."

I took a couple of deep breaths and noticed my hands were shaking like a pine tree's needles in a tornado.

"A dear old friend of mine, Chaung Tsu, once said, 'I dreamed I was a butterfly and when I woke I didn't know if I was a man who dreamed he was a butterfly or if I was a butterfly who was dreaming he was a man.'"

"So what the hell does that mean?"

"Go back to sleep and in the morning you will remember your dream and you can tell me."

I lay back down and couldn't get the words out of my head, 'If you meet the Buddha on the road, kill him.' Kill the Buddha? Was Pooh the Buddha? That was what the dream was telling me I had to do. Now I have killed squirrels, possums, pigs, deer, ducks, and I even shot a turtle one time when Chigger and I were thirteen and been drinking some white lightning we'd stolen from Mr. Brown the county bootlegger. I'd never killed a man, though I sure have wanted to a time or two and they may have deserved it. I never thought of offing someone I knew and admired. Oh hell, it was just a dream, I reckon. Besides, I wasn't sure Pooh was the Buddha, though I have to admit, based on what ole Jim told me about Buddhism, I guess he could be. But then again, how could he be? The Buddha is too important to visit Scottsboro, Alabama. Maybe San Francisco or New York, but Alabama?

# Chapter 19

The next morning Pooh was sitting in a chair meditating. "Would you like to tell me about your dreams?" he said, as he opened his eyes and placed his hands in his lap.

"I dreamed about Dolly Parton—you know, the country singer with the huge rack and the big hair. She was leading a llama."

Pooh laughed. "The Dalai Llama!"

"Yeah, that's what I said."

"Me and Billy were in a garden, and when she would speak to a seed it growed into a vegetable and Billy disappeared and became a huge sunflower." I didn't tell him the killing a Buddha part.

"Sounds like a good dream to me. Was there more?"

I told him what Dolly said to Billy, but I was afraid to tell him the rest. "Pooh, when someone tells you in a dream to do something, are you supposed to do it?"

Pooh looked at me for a moment. "The Talmud says, 'An uninterrupted dream is like an unopened letter.' The key is to get the dream interpreted. Let me know if I can help."

"How about we get started on Billy's garden?" was all I could think of to say at the moment.

I gave Pooh a pair of overalls I picked up at the seed store for him to put on, 'cause he couldn't work in his pajama-looking outfit.

Grace said she would wash the pajamas while he worked in the overalls. Then I went to the shed where they kept the Troy-Bilt tiller, gardening tools, mulch, and other stuff we'd need. I took all the tools out to the place the garden had been in years past. It wasn't very big, maybe three-quarters of an acre, more or less. I figured it would take a little more than two days to put it in. Grace was ready to go and when Pooh came out in his overalls we both could barely keep ourselves from busting out laughing. It didn't seem to bother him a bit.

"All right, Pooh, here's the deal. I'm going to crank up the tiller and show you how to break the ground." She fired right up, and I plowed a few feet as Pooh watched. I had him take it and boy hidey that damn tiller damn near drug his fat ass all over that little garden and by the time he finally figured out how to not let it he was huffing and puffing, completely out of breath.

Grace came over and took it from him. "Pooh, you better help Bubba pulverize the ground a little and I'll finish breaking it up." She knew what she was doing as good as I did, if not better. Pooh and I took our hoes by the flat side and pounded the earth. When Grace was finished she went into the house and brought out a boom box and sat it down on the picnic table by the garden and put on a John Prine CD.

"Blow up your TV . . . build you a home . . . eat a lot of peaches, try and find Jesus on your own . . ." As the song was playing, Grace brought us some cold lemonade. The sun hit her just right, where she was standing, and I could see right through her gauzy hippy shirt though I tried not to stare. I couldn't help myself, so I said a prayer right there silently, "Dear God in heaven, please help me find a good juke joint tonight and the courage to ask this beautiful woman to go dancing. Oh yeah, and for her to answer yes. In Jesus' name, Amen."

We had our lemonade and mulched the garden. The smell of fresh-turned earth and pine mulch was comforting. The raised beds had railroad ties about two feet high wrapping the black earth. Mulching was an all-day job. By the time we finished we were sweaty, dirty, and tired, but satisfied with the results. Afterwards, Pooh went to the guest house to meditate or take a nap (they kinda look the same to me sometimes).

Grace and I sat underneath a hundred-and-something-year-old oak tree. It was a big'un. "Grace, do you remember your dreams?"

She blinked at me. "Why yes I do. Most folks don't take dreams seriously, but I have for a long time. Why do you ask?"

"Well, ever since I've been traveling with Pooh I've had a lot of crazy-ass dreams, and up until now I never dreamed much and I certainly didn't remember them. How do you know what they mean?"

"Sometimes I know what mine mean, but I don't think other people can tell you what your dreams mean. But I had a good one last night. You want me to tell it to you?"

"You bet."

"Last night I dreamed this good-looking man and I were dancing up a storm. I haven't been dancing in a long time and I know this little place over in Muscle Shoals that has a great band. If you'll take me tonight it sure would be nice."

"Praise the Lord and pass the ammunition. My prayers have been answered. Yeah, I'll take you." I was tickled pink.

"Great! I'll get cleaned up and fix us some supper and we'll have us an adventure tonight."

I got me a shower, put on some smell-good that I found in the medicine cabinet, and slid into my new western shirt and Wrangler jeans Grace bought at Cold Water Feed and Seed, same time I got Pooh his overalls and garden stuff that Grace paid for and said I could pay her back when I got some work again. Don't mean to brag, but I looked as good as I ever did. I smiled at myself in the mirror and said, "You go get 'er, you good-looking son-of-a-bitch."

# Chapter 20

Just as Grace and me were getting into the van, Pooh walked up. "May I go with you?"

"Sure, we would love to have you," Grace said.

I remembered my dream from the night before, where the Dalai llama said, 'If you meet the Buddha on the road, kill him.' At that moment I thought it was a pretty good idea. Two is company, but taking a Buddha along with you to a bar was just fucked up. He got in and off we went.

We pulled into the gravel parking lot of the Stagger Lee's Lounge and there must have been a hundred trucks and two cars.

"I think you both will like this place. It has great music and a real friendly atmosphere," Grace said as she took my hand and Pooh's. We walked in and boy hidey, the country band was cooking, beer was flowing, and rednecks were dancing up a storm. Everybody was behaving themselves since it was only about nine o'clock. We sat down at a table and Pooh was looking around taking it all in.

"Pooh, you look like you've never been to a place like this before," Grace said.

"You're right. I haven't. This is an amazing place. Everyone looks so happy here." About that time a waitress came up to take our order. "What'll you have, Sugar?" she said, her eyes on Pooh.

"No, I don't think I want sugar," he said serious like.

She looked at Pooh for a minute and then laughed. "Aren't you 'bout the cutest thing these eyes have seen in a while."

Pooh blushed a little and Grace giggled.

"So, what will you folks have from the bar?"

"I'll have a Buddha, I mean a Bud in a bottle, and bring 'Sugar' here one and this lovely lady one too," I said.

"Three Buds coming right up," she said. "Now, you have yourself a good time, Sugar, and if you need anything at all my name is Sandy. All you have to do is ask," she winked at Pooh and then at Grace.

Sandy brought the beers. As we all took our first few swallows, the lead singer in the band yelled, "Crank her up." Everybody from Alabama knows what those words mean, and they started playing our national sacred anthem, "Sweet Home Alabama."

"You want to dance?" Grace leaned in towards me.

Man, was Grace a fine dancer. I looked like a spastic having a seizure, but the more Buds I put in me the less I cared.

We'd been there about an hour, and Pooh just drank one beer after another like it was water. I told him he'd better slow down, but I figured as big as he was he could hold a lot. Finally, he looked at Grace and said, "I'm ready to learn how to dance."

She took Pooh's hand and led him out to the dance floor. Now if you want to see a sight you ought to see a big, half-drunk Asian guy in black pj's line dancing. He may be smart and know things before they happen, but he has less natural rhythm than any white guy you've ever seen. Lord did he look like he was having the time of his life out there, or at least until he started cutting in on every guy on the dance floor and slow dancing with their women even during a fast song. Finally, he cut in on the wrong peckerwood

that'd had at least as many beers as Pooh. The fella wouldn't give up
his woman, who was real big. Hell, she was almost as big as Pooh,
with bleached blond hair and a skintight leopard-print miniskirt.
Pooh looked like the big love bug had bitten him pretty hard. He
tried to cut in a second time, and the fella who looked like a string
bean compared to Pooh pushed Pooh's hand away from his shoulder. "Get your own woman, goddamnit! Now get. Shew, go away,
asshole." He turned his back on Pooh and tried to ignore him. Pooh
tapped him again on the shoulder, and this time the guy faced him
and Pooh got into one of those Sumo wrestler positions and started charging towards the string bean and bumped him real hard and
the guy hit the floor. He got up and charged at Pooh the way you
tackle a guy with the football. "You cocksucker, I told you to get
your own woman. I'm going to mess you up, man." Pooh turned to
the side and the guy ran straight into the wall and bounced off it
like he was a rubber ball before falling to the floor. The third time
he got up he pulled a Buck knife out of his pocket and started coming towards Pooh. "I'm going to cut your balls off."

I thought this guy was gonna kill my Buddha and I couldn't let
that happen; at least not until I knew what it meant in my dream.
It didn't say if someone else tries to kill the Buddha to let them. If
Pooh was the Buddha I knew I had to be the one, so I jumped up
from the table and came between the skinny guy and Pooh. "You're
going to have to go through me first." I was hoping I sounded real
tough and he'd back off 'cause I didn't want to fight him. I hate
to fight, but I will when push comes to shove . . . and damn if he
didn't push me and shove me so I got all over him like a duck on a
June bug and we wrestled around on the floor. One of his buddies
jumped in and tried to hold me, but Pooh bumped him half way
across the bar and into a bunch of tables. Then some girl came over
and pulled my hair. Grace jumped on her back and tried to pull

her off of me. Finally, the bartender pulled out a sawed-off shotgun and fired it at the ceiling. That pretty much brought everything to a screeching halt.

"Let's get the hell out of here," I said, wiping the blood from several places. "We sure had a good time, didn't we?"

Dang, it was good being around my people again. Best cut-and-shoot bar I'd been to in a long time.

# Chapter 21

We all sort of fell into the van. I had a cut lip and a knot on my noggin but Pooh didn't have a scratch on him. Grace's hair was messed up and her blouse was torn but nothing serious.

"Pooh, how in the tarnation did you make those guys fly through the air without breaking a sweat?" I had to ask.

Pooh looked sleepy-eyed, "The point is not to harm your opponent but to re-direct and transform his aggression. Ultimately, you use their own energy and momentum against them. This way they learn that violence will turn against the one using it."

As soon as Pooh said that he fell asleep. Me and Grace were wide awake and mostly sober. "What do you say we clear our heads before heading home," I said to Grace.

"Sounds good. Let's go to Florence and Wilson Dam and watch the river. Maybe we'll see some towboats lock through."

When we got there Pooh was still sound asleep. The night was clear and there was a full moon as we walked to the dam. You could hear the water pouring over the dam and the sound of a towboat horn coming into the lock. There are these little islands down below formed around these huge rocks; the water crashes into them with all the power of God. We were the only ones there. We went down to the end of the dam, leaned against the guardrail, and looked at the view without saying a word for a long time.

"I sure enjoyed tonight," Grace said. "Well at least most of it. I know this sounds corny but it feels like I've known both of you much longer than I have. You both have this familiar feeling. I don't know how to explain it. Do you know what I mean?" She stared off into space.

"Yeah, I know. I've never had this feeling before. It's like I've known Pooh forever and now I feel that way about you. Spooky, ain't it?"

Grace turned towards me and I knew it was time. I kissed her right on the mouth but not like I ever kissed my two wives or others in-between. It was soft and hard at the same time, like I was saying hello and good-bye.

I told her this and she said, "What does that mean?"

"I don't know. I mean it was soft like and real tender. Shirley, my ex-wife, used to say I kissed like a vacuum cleaner."

We held onto each other the way people do when they are going off to war. Finally, I stopped and pulled away. "There is a lot you don't know about me, Grace. I've been married twice and am in the process of getting a divorce from my second. I've never been a good husband and I suck as a father. I have two women and a grown son that pretty much hate my guts. I don't want to add another woman to that list. You're a good woman and you deserve a hell of a lot better man than me. So I think we'd better put the quietus on this whole thing right here and now." I started toward the van, my feet feeling as heavy as cement.

"You wait a minute. We're not done talking!" She yelled at my back. I turned around and walked back to the railing.

"You think you are the only one that has a past?" she said. "Why do you think I'm not married? It's not because I haven't had opportunities. I'm in my thirties and there still hasn't been a ring on this finger or a bun in the oven. Most of the men around here are just not interested in what I want and need from a man. Now I don't know what you were like before but watching you around my brother, overcoming your fears and all and how you are with Pooh tells me something in you is changing and changing pretty damn fast for a fella from Scottsboro, Alabama, or any place in Alabama as far as that goes. Don't get me wrong, I'm not proposing marriage; I'm just asking you not to walk away from something that feels special and right. Now come here and kiss me one more time and make it a good one. No more disparaging remarks, I need to get home. We still have a garden to put in early tomorrow."

I kissed her as best as I knew how. Her words were as sweet as her kisses and I knew I was falling in love with this woman 'cause of who she was and what she believes. I'd fallen in love plenty of times but most of my relationships, well let's just say I've had colds last longer than most of them, because I didn't really like them as people. But then again I didn't much like myself as a person for that matter.

# Chapter 22

The next morning I was up real early and I just sat on the porch with my coffee listening to katydids, crickets, and an owl. I just sat real still and felt the wind blow against my face. I was glad no one else was up. I was hoping that I wouldn't remember any dreams and just as I thought that to myself I remembered one. The skinny guy that Pooh and I fought with was in it, and he was sitting on the floor with his first finger and thumb meditating like Pooh. I came into the room and he opened his eyes and said, "Remember, if you meet the Buddha on the road, kill him. You should continue doing this until you receive a clear indication, for example in your dreams, that your unwholesome deeds have been purified. And the next time you or Pu Tai comes into a bar, I'm going to kick both your sorry asses." Then he shot me the bird. Talk about your mixed messages.

I thought about it and thought about what killing the Buddha meant and what Grace said to me last night and I didn't know what to make of either. Just as the sun came up I started thinking of my boy and the fight we had and how we'd always fought nearly every time we laid eyes on each other. Sometimes the look in his eyes would be like the one I had when I'd look at my own father—you know the look that could kill. About that time Pooh joined me on the porch.

"Pooh, I've got to clean up my unwholesome deeds with my ex-wives but especially my son."

"Trust me. I know this. How do you propose to do this?" Pooh looked me straight in the eye, and when he did all I saw was tenderness. Now don't get me wrong, I wasn't going gay on him or anything. It's just I'd never seen a man look at me that way.

"I don't know. I'm going into the main house and I'm going to call his mother and get his number and call him I reckon. Do you think that's a good idea?"

"I know your son has a short fuse like your dad. But he's not your dad and you're not your dad. Now I only got a little time left to complete the mission the Wise Ones sent me on, so I hope you will hurry."

Tom was in the kitchen with Grace and he was crying and sobbing. I came into the house to make a call, but thought about turning around and making it later. I didn't because Pooh had impressed upon me the need to get going. Grace was holding Tom as Tom kept saying, "He's going faster than I thought he would. God, what am I going to do without him? It's too soon. We have so much more we want to do together."

"It's okay, Tom, just let it out. I'm here." She started sobbing and I didn't know what to do, so I went into the living room to call my ex. My hand started shaking as I dialed her number. It seemed like everybody was losing it. Hell, even Pooh got in a brawl. What's this world coming to?

# Chapter 23

"Hello Shirley, yeah it's me. Don't hang up. No I haven't been drinking. I've been doing a lot of thinking about Lucius and well I have to purify my unwholesome deeds."

"You're what needs purifying!" She sounded exasperated. "Are you sure you aren't drunk?"

"I need to make things right with me and my son. Lots of things have happened in the last week or so, and well I . . . how can I get in touch with him?"

She didn't sound like she bought my change of heart, but she gave me his phone number and said he was living in the mountains over in Mentone, Alabama, which is about thirty or forty minutes from Scottsboro but in many ways not much like the rest of Alabama. She told me that he would be leaving Mentone to go to Europe on tour with some big-name rock-and-roll band and he was leaving the day after tomorrow and that he'd be gone for at least a year. He told her he was seriously thinking about staying in London, because he'd met a woman the last time he was over there that he liked very much.

My son is a musician. I guess I forgot to mention that. He's a pretty good one too, but one of the things he and I would always argue about is the question of how he planned to make a decent living with his music. I kept telling him to get a real job with good benefits and he could play his music on the side. He would argue that he'd make it and that maybe if I had ever done what I loved I wouldn't be the miserable son-of-a-bitch that I am. I'd tell him the same thing my daddy told me, "What does love have to do with what you do for a living?" He always said, "I never loved a day at work, but I did it to put food on the table, a roof over your head, and clothes on your back." I hated hearing that shit and I ended up saying the same kind of crap to Lucius, except it was his momma who took care of those things for him a hell of a lot better than I did. I called Lucius and got his answering machine, so I didn't leave a message. I didn't know what to say, so I hung up. By the time I got back into the kitchen Tom had left and Grace was still drying her eyes. I walked over to her, "Are you all right?"

"Billy is slipping every day now. I don't know how much longer he has and Tom's heart is just breaking. Goddamn AIDS. Goddamn government for not making it a priority to cure. Goddamn God for . . . for . . . just Goddamn Him for the whole mess."

She was pissed off more than sad now, but I held her real tight anyway and she started crying again.

"We got to get to the garden." She headed for the door wiping her tears with her shirtsleeve.

Pooh was already out there, and he looked like he was talking to someone or I guess himself, which wouldn't surprise me none. "Who you talking to Pooh?" I asked.

"Just the garden and the Wise Ones."

"Pooh, we have to leave today. We can't finish the garden. I've had these weird dreams, and well I've got to get to Mentone, which is almost three hours from here. My son is leaving the country, day after tomorrow. I need to see him before he goes. I got to set things right with him."

"I know you do. And we will leave in the morning. There is plenty of time. Trust me, first things first."

I thought about the Dalai dream again. I was pretty mad at Pooh for insisting that we stay, but what was I gonna do. I had to start trusting somebody, someday.

Although it was certainly a pretty day to begin a garden, it was clouded by my thoughts. I knew this was important to Billy and Pooh and even Grace, so I thought, a job worth doing is worth doing well. "Okay, let's do this. We're going to put in some sweet corn about an inch deep. They will come up in five to ten days. We'll put in the radish seeds about a quarter-inch deep and they should be up in about five days."

Pooh looked at me like he was impressed or proud or something. "How long do things take?" he asked.

"Well let's see, a lot depends on air and water and condition of the soil. One thing is how much air and water lie in the spaces between the soil particles. The soil is pretty good here for quick growth. It has a lot of natural fertility because of all the organic stuff they've been putting on it all year. Some folks say that cleanliness is next to godliness, but I think it starts here in the garden. Soil-borne diseases, weed seeds, and other pests hitch a ride on dirty shoes, tools, containers, hoses, and stuff like that. The cleaner it is the healthier the plants, which attract fewer problems than those that have poor nutrition and poor growing conditions."

Pooh looked at me for a minute then grabbed a handful of corn seeds and let them flow from one hand to the other.

"I didn't know all of this, but so far what you say seems to apply to humans as well. Don't you agree?"

"If you say so. Now any weeds you see pull them up. Like my granddaddy used to tell me, 'Son, weeds are just plants that grow where you don't want them to.' Main thing to remember is put the right plants in the right place. You got to know where the sun shines and the shadows fall at different times of the day."

Grace looked at me sweetly. "Seems you know a good bit about gardening. I'm impressed."

"Not that much really. Mostly what my granddaddy taught me and what I picked up along the way. He always saw his garden as a small part of the bigger world and understood that the way he gardened reflected how he loved the Lord and his wife and tried to love his children, though I reckon he was better at gardening than fathering."

"Maybe you can change that legacy," Pooh said.

"Maybe. Now let's plant these sunflowers over here in the corner." I pointed to the right side of the plot. "You know some plants naturally grow better in the company of other plants. Sometimes one plant keeps the pests off the others and attracts your good insects that attack its companion's pests. What you want to do is mix them up a good bit and that way one helps the other."

"So master gardeners promote diversity in their gardens, is that what you're saying?" asked Grace.

"I reckon."

# Chapter 24

I showed Pooh and Grace where I thought everything should go. I stepped off the space that would be the rows and ran string down where the plants should go.

She looked at me like some kind of seed was growing in her heart.

"I'm going to tell Billy what seeds we were planting and see if there were others he wanted me to include," I said, not able to let her look at me that way any longer. I didn't know what to do.

I walked down the hallway to his bedroom and his door was open. I thought he might be asleep so I was real quiet like. As I got closer I heard him talking. I didn't know anybody else was in the house, so I poked my head in the door and saw him kneeling by his bed. His hands were clasped together and his eyes were closed. I figured he was praying to God, though I didn't understand why, given he was gay and all and I was pretty sure the man upstairs was turning a deaf ear to whatever he might be saying. I caught the last few words, "I seek your kingdom God first and to become one with you. If it be your will then all things—wisdom, abundance, and health will be added to me as a part of my divine birthright, since I am made in your image. Beloved Christ, I know that I am not the body, not the blood, not the energy, not my thoughts, and my cells are made of light and that light permeates the dark nooks of my bodily sickness. In Christ's name I pray. Amen." Billy looked up and saw me and I didn't know what to do. I sort of acted like I didn't hear him, but I'm sure he saw the confusion on my face.

"Do you think because I'm gay, I shouldn't pray?" he said as he struggled to pull himself up. "Would you mind giving me a hand?"

"Do you really think he listens to your prayers and that you can change his mind and that he will cure your AIDS?" I asked.

"Bubba, I don't pray to change his mind. I pray to change mine."

"Well, if you say so. Listen, for what it's worth, I have no right to judge anybody about anything. I hope, I mean, oh hell, I just came in to tell you what I've planted in your garden and to ask if there is anything else you wanted. We have to leave first thing in the morning. I got to go see my son, so if you want something in there, now is the time."

"I didn't know you had a son. What's his name?"

"Lucius. He's twenty-one or two this month."

"I have a son the same age. He'll be twenty in February." Billy reached for a picture of him on the table beside the bed. I'd seen it before but never guessed it was his son.

"You have a son?"

"Yes. I was married a long time ago. Me and his mother are still real good friends, and my son comes over at least once a week. He's a fine man." You could hear the pride in his voice.

"Does he, mind that you are, you know?" I stuttered.

"Oh, do you mean sick, dying, or gay?" he grinned. "No he doesn't mind the gay part."

"My son hates my guts and I ain't even gay. We barely speak to each other and haven't for a long time. But I'm going to go see him before he leaves the country. He's a musician and is going on tour and has a little girlfriend over in England. I don't know why I'm telling you all of this."

"Maybe, because you need someone to listen. I'm not going anywhere at the moment if you want to tell me more."

I pulled up a chair beside his bed and I told him about my two ex's and all about Lucius or at least all I knew to tell and about how I came to be with Pooh, and how I was becoming more and more convinced he was the Buddha. I also confessed I was having these different kinds of feelings for his sister. This went on for about an hour or two. He just listened to me rattle on and on and never interrupted me once or gave me any advice or anything. I couldn't believe I was talking like this to anyone. Rednecks don't talk about such things to anyone, much less a gay guy. But sure enough, that's exactly what I did. I talked my head off and felt gooder than hell for doing so. And I don't rightly care who knows I did or what they think about it.

After I finished airing my dirty laundry out to a stranger, Billy looked at me real kindly like. "You're a lot better man than you think you are and you are not your dad. You still have a chance to, maybe not be the father your son needed when he was a boy, but be the friend he could use as a man." I can't thank you enough for the garden. Will I see you before you leave in the morning?"

"I reckon. I hope you are right about the father stuff, and I guess we'll see. I hope you get better. Thank you for listening to me and for what you just said."

Billy dozed off and I slipped out of the room as quietly as I could.

# Chapter 25

By the time I got back to the garden, Pooh and Grace were just about finishing up. You should have seen them smiling at each other and then at me when they saw me. "I think we're about done. Looks good, doesn't it?" I said as I started picking up the tools to take back to the shed.

"You've done a good thing for my brother, Bubba," Grace said as she kissed me flush on my mouth. Talk about making me smile and look real toothy.

"I think your brother did a real good thing for him." Pooh glanced at me. "Didn't he, Bubba?"

I turned red and looked at the floor.

"Now it is time to get cleaned up, eat, sleep, and be on our way to Mentone to clean up the mess between you and your son and plant a few new seeds."

"I'm going to fix you fellas a meal fit for kings because that's exactly what you are to me," said Grace as she headed for the house.

We finished picking up the gardening tools and leftover bags of seeds. Pooh and I took our time going to the guest cottage.

Once inside, Pooh looked at me. "Sit down, Bubba, and tell me about your visit with Billy."

"Oh, hell, you already know what happened," I said.

"Yes, but I'd like to hear it from your mouth."

"All right. Billy is, well, he's all right. He seems like a good man. I wish he wasn't, you know—but since he is, well, he's all right and I'm sad that he's dying."

"Bubba, you're a better man than you think. Billy knows it, Grace knows it, and I know it. All we can hope for is that someday you know it and that your son finds it out and you find out that he's a good man as well before it is too late.

"Yeah," I said as I looked at the clock.

"Speaking of late, we better get going or we're going to be late for our kingly supper," Pooh said as he placed his hand on top of my head like you see the Pope do when he wants to bestow a blessing or something and I didn't mind.

"Thanks for what you just said, Pooh. I've never heard that from another man."

"Trust me. I know good men when I see them. Now let us proceed to do one of my favorite things in the world—eat. I love your people's country cooking. I especially like how everything is fried—vegetables, and the meat. I love it." Pooh patted his stomach. "We'll eat, spend a little time with Billy, Grace, and Tom, get a good night's sleep, and be off first thing in the morning. You have only two days to get to your son and turn things around."

I hadn't seen a whole lot of Tom 'cause he'd been at work mostly since me and Pooh got there. "Anybody want a beer? I don't mind if I do," said Tom, not waiting for anyone to answer. The more he drank the more talkative he got. "You know AIDS sucks? I mean, why can't we cure the modern black plague of our time?" He took a few moments and then downed a whole beer without stopping and then headed to the liquor cabinet. "If God hates queers so much, why did he give us the ability to love in the first goddamn place? Who does he think he is? He gives us love and then takes it away from us just like that." Tom tried to snap his fingers, but he kept missing them.

"Tom, let me make you some coffee," Grace said as she took Tom's drink.

No one knew how many he'd had, but everyone was feeling that if something wasn't done pretty quickly it could turn ugly, from the way he was talking. He wouldn't give her the drink and instead tipped his glass back, downed it, and poured another straight vodka before he turned to me. "Look at you. You got your health. I know for a fact you got a son and he's probably just as healthy as you are. You got the hots for my sister-in-law and you got this big man here," he put his arm around Pooh, "to help you learn how to be a goddamn human being instead of the redneck you and I know you are. You hate us gay people and probably like every other redneck in this stinking state, that I was born and raised in, think we should just all die with AIDS so you won't have to deal with your own homophobia."

Before Tom finished I walked over to him. "Listen, you better sober up. I'm not my friend here," I pointed to Pooh, "and I'll whup ass if you don't stop this bullshit right now."

Grace looked at Tom and then at me. "Boys, boys, could we just lower the testosterone level just a bit here. Now everyone just take a couple of deep breaths. This is our last night together before you two have to leave," she pointed at Pooh and me. "We don't know how much time my brother has, but I know him well enough to know he wouldn't want anything like this going on."

Tom sank into the couch and started crying. Pooh sat beside him, took his hands in his, and just held them for several moments. Then he rubbed his hands together real fast and real hard like he was warming them up or something. He put his hands over Tom's eyes, then over his ears, and then his mouth, and then his heart.

After a few moments on his heart, Pooh clapped his hands, and Tom looked at me. "Please forgive me Bubba, I didn't mean what I said." He was as sober as a judge.

Pooh came over to me and I recoiled.

There was something in Tom's behavior that triggered the mean in me. I think he reminded me of my father or something so I yelled at Pooh. "No, don't touch me. I'm tired of this goddamn game we're playing; you're an illusion, a hallucination, and a figment of my imagination!"

Then he did the Dog Whisperer on my ass, "Shhhhhhh." He snapped his fingers and I lay down on the rug and showed him my belly, and he rubbed his hands real hard for a few moments and then he placed them on my eyes, ears, mouth, and heart and clapped. And for just a moment I felt, like, well, I felt like, like something came out of me or went into me. Oh, hell, I don't know what I'm talking about or what I felt but I know I'd never felt anything like that before.

We ate and didn't say much of anything. Everyone was serious, except for Pooh who was as happy as always. Tom was asleep on the couch and looked as peaceful as a newborn. As I was helping Grace clean up the dishes, Pooh went into Billy's room.

"I'm glad it didn't go any further with you and Tom. I don't mean to make excuses for him but he's exhausted emotionally and physically. The last six months or so has drained as much life out of him as it has Billy. We both are having a terrible time accepting that we have to let him go. But I was real proud of you for not getting into it with him any more than you did."

"I am too. I hate to fight. I always have. But where I came from if you didn't fight, well let's just say you had to or else."

"Like I've told you, I know how you were brought up. We're all from the South, well except Pooh, who must be from a little bit of everywhere I guess. Why don't you go in and say good-bye to Billy while I finish up here in the kitchen and then if you're not too tired, I want to take you someplace that's real special to me to say my good-byes." She looked tired and hurtin' and peaceful all at the same time. And me, I didn't know whether to shit or go blind. I mean what the hell am I supposed to do with all these strange people? But I realized it was important to say good-bye to her brother.

I walked in real quiet like and as I got into the room Billy said, "Pooh, you have to talk to Tom and Grace. I need you to get them to see that they have to let me go. I'm ready. I'm in terrible pain and the pain of seeing them see me in pain is killing my soul. You have to make them see they have to let me go. Promise you will do this for me. Promise!"

Pooh looked at me and then back at Billy while stroking Billy's forehead and hair. "Trust me. I'll help them to see this first thing in the morning because Tom has had a real hard night and is already asleep. Bubba and I are going to bathe you and get you ready for bed so you can get some sleep and dream about the place that you will be going soon." Pooh motioned for me to come over. "Bubba, I want you to help me bathe this man."

"Pooh, I don't know. You're asking too damn much of me. I mean I've stayed here, I've put in his garden, I've talked to him and he's listened real good to me, but bathing a man, I just can't go there Pooh, I'm sorry."

"I understand. This is all new for you. How about I bathe him and you just get a pan of warm water, some soap, and a cloth and wash his feet. I'll take care of the rest of him."

"Pooh, I don't know."

"I know you are from people who do this."

I thought to myself he was talking about how people over on

Sand Mountain where my ancestors hail from are often referred to
as 'foot-washin Baptists' though I hadn't seen anyone do that in a
while I guess because we were becoming so sophisticated and all.

"Okay. All right. I'll wash his feet."

Pooh leaned towards me and kissed me right on the forehead
and I didn't even bother to wipe it off but I wasn't about to kiss
him back. I got the pan and soap and stuff, and I took off Billy's
socks. His feet were thin and delicate like a little girl's and as white
as cotton, but they didn't smell or anything like that. I watched as
Pooh gently took the sponge and patted him so gently with it, oc-
casionally stroking his head and hair again and again. I rolled up
my sleeves and I remembered how my granddaddy would come in
from plowing his fields or tending to his huge chicken houses and
grandma would fix him a pan of water just like the one I had for
Billy. Granddaddy would soak his feet for a while. On Saturday
nights we'd watch wrestling on television and after a while Grandma would come in and take a towel and dry his feet. At that moment I felt a tear or two run down my eyes before I realized I was
drying Billy's feet, and I didn't know if I was tearing up for remembering Grandma and Granddaddy or Billy, or me or the tenderness
I saw in Pooh. Maybe it was all of it.

When I got finished and was putting on a fresh pair of socks
for Billy, Pooh just looked at me in a way I can't explain. It was a
look I had never seen before, a look no one had ever given me before. A look that I didn't know what to do with.

"Your humble Jesus washed the feet of the poor and sick and
the low. I always loved that about him. Now you run on and go be
with Grace and say your good-byes. I'll take it from here," Pooh
said as he waved his hand at me. "Tomorrow morning we'll have a
ceremony and we'll be off to Mentone."

# Chapter 26

Grace was standing in the vestibule with her car keys, a quilt, and a bottle of wine. "Are you ready?"

"You bet. Let's get out of here. Where are we going?" I still had some wetness around my eyes, and I turned my head from her so she wouldn't see.

"My special place. No one will be there this time of night," she said, locking her arm in mine as she escorted me to the van.

As we drove through the dark into the TVA reservation with its turns and twists, we didn't see one car. Mostly we talked about the garden and a little about what happened, but not much. I think she wanted to keep it light as much as I did. Truth be told, I felt like I'd been rode hard and put up wet and I just couldn't take too much more intensity.

She parked on a dirt road and we walked down the trail. The large Maglite she carried let us see the area real good. We ended up at this clearing where you could see the Tennessee River and the bridge that connected Sheffield to Florence. It was a clear night with a full moon, so we could see the spill waves crashing over the dam like they were in a hurry to get somewhere.

"Next to my beehives this is my favorite spot," she said as she spread the quilt. "My grandmother made this quilt when she was sixteen. She gave it to me when I turned sixteen and I've had it on my bed ever since, but never anyplace else, certainly not on the ground. I've been saving it for a special occasion like this one."

"I don't know what to say. It's beautiful. What's so special about this occasion?"

"You are," she said, as we sat down and I put my arms around her. She nestled into me the way I'd seen kittens scrooch up to their mother. I held her real tight.

"Just look at that water," I said, marveling at the moon's soft rippled reflection.

She said, "When I die I want my ashes spread on that river, because I know it flows all the way to paradise and my granny, and if God ain't there it will be all right with me just so long as they are." She waved her arm the way I'd seen magicians do when they wanted something to appear.

"I've always wanted my ashes to be scattered on this river. I can't believe you do, too. Most Christians don't think that's right," I said, running my fingers over the patterns in the quilt.

I turned her face towards mine and I kissed her very slowly and then she said, "Hold me, hold me and never let me go. Make love to me like I've never been made love to before."

I pulled off my shirt and she took off her blouse. I took off her jeans and she took off mine, and every time something came off it was like a layer of my skin was peeling off one layer at a time, one heartbreak at a time, one failed love at a time. For just a moment it seemed like my past had been stripped away. By the time we were laying on that purple, wedding-ring quilt made from rag and remnants, pieces of other people's shirts and dresses, we were lost in the time we had left. I don't know how long I descended into her and she came into me and when we couldn't take it any longer. We held each other and both of us wept for a long time. It was the strangest experience I'd ever had. But it didn't scare me at all. Finally we sat up and watched the river and just listened to each other's breathing.

"Grace, there's something that I should tell you. It has been wanting to come out for a long time and I've never told anyone before and I don't know the words to use but bear with me. I'm afraid that, shit, I'm afraid that there is something in me that's so broken that it can never be fixed and that if it ain't fixed then I can't ever be the kind of man a woman like you needs. That's why I've either been alone or been with women that I know I'm only going to be with a short time before one of us leaves. Sometimes that is why I think I left Lucius. If I stayed around him too long that which is broken in me would break him, and I couldn't stand myself if I did that to my son. My second wife, Ginger, wanted children real bad, but every time we had sex I'd pray to God that she didn't get pregnant and she never did. God probably didn't want that broken thing passed on any more than I did. I don't know how to be with people, a woman, a gay couple, or even my own son. So tomorrow when I leave I want you to forget I was ever here and I want you to find yourself the kind of man that deserves you, though I'm never going to forget this night as long as I live. I'm going to say good-bye and that will be that."

Grace started crying and I held her and we sat there for about another hour and then it started pouring down rain. We ran for the van and by the time we got there we were soaking wet. We drove home chilled to the bone.

When we pulled into the driveway she grabbed my arm before I could open the door. "I'm not going to accept what you are saying. I've waited my whole life for you to come along and now that you are here you can't just say you are afraid you are broken. If you are, then get yourself fixed, get some help, some counseling or whatever, but we are meant to be together and that's all there is to it. I'm not taking no for an answer," she said in between teeth chattering. "And if you ever have another child, they will have a great father. You'll do it better the next time around."

# Chapter 27

The next morning, Pooh was already up and dressed and over at the main house with Tom and Grace. None of us were looking each other in the eye or saying anything.

As we ate our breakfast, the tension and tiredness seemed to be spread out through the room like kudzu. It swallowed everyone whole. Even Pooh wasn't totally immune. We all spoke in short sentences—"Pass the butter," "Biscuits are ready," "Anybody want more coffee?"

At last, Pooh inhaled deeply and said, "It's time."

"Time for what?" Tom said in between sips of coffee.

"To say good-bye to Billy," he pointed towards the bedroom.

We all held our breaths and just looked at Pooh.

"This is what Billy asked me to do before Bubba and I left this morning. Shall we proceed into the room?" Pooh got up and headed for the bedroom and we all fell in behind him without anyone saying a word of objection.

"I want you to form a circle around the bed and take each other's hands. Tom, you stand over there on the left side, Grace on the right, and Bubba and I will be in the middle."

Billy took Tom's and Grace's hands, Pooh took her hand, I took his, and I took Tom's with my left hand. Billy started shedding a few tears, as did Grace and Tom and Pooh. Pooh closed his eyes. "A man traveling across a field encountered a tiger. He ran and the tiger ran after him. The man came to the edge of a cliff. He was tired and could not run any farther, so he took hold of a vine and swung himself over the edge. The tiger sniffed at him from above. Trembling and full of fear, the man looked down to where, far below, another tiger was waiting to eat him. Only the vine kept him from falling. He looked up and he saw two mice, one white and one black, nibbling at the vine. The man then looked and saw a luscious strawberry near him. Grasping the vine with one hand, he plucked the strawberry with the other and then he let go. As he fell all he could think about was how sweet that strawberry tasted." Pooh opened his eyes and looked at Tom and Grace.

Billy wiped the tears from his eyes and smiled. "It's time to let me go. I need you to let me go. I've done what I am supposed to do here. Tom, I have loved you more than anyone in my life. You have been my life and I have let you love me, something I have never let happen before with the exception of my dear sister." He turned towards Grace, "And sweetie, it's time to let me go. You have been the greatest sister and friend a man could ever hope for. Please take care of yourself. Have a wonderful life with some man." He looked at me as he said that, and then back at Grace. "Look in on Tom when you can and help him keep the garden going when you come to visit him from wherever you end up. Tell Mom and Dad I love them and that I understand." Again, he looked at me and then at Tom. "Tom, you keep an eye on my sister and don't you live alone. You're no damn good at being alone, and you know I know it." He took a couple of real shallow breaths.

"It's not time yet. You can't go," Tom whispered. "We have so much more to do. Don't we?" He laid his head on Billy's chest as if to listen to his last remaining breaths. "Good-bye, dear one. I got to let you go," Tom said calmly and kissed him on the lips.

Grace put her head next to Billy's heart. "Good-bye brother, I need to let you go." And with that Billy looked into Pooh's eyes and then mine and then Grace's and finally Tom's, and he took a deep breath, made the sign of the cross, and he was gone.

Pooh motioned for me to follow him out of the room. We left as quiet as we could and Tom and Grace took each other's hands and were praying. I had almost forgotten that I only had two days left before my son left the country and just as I was thinking that to myself, Pooh said, "Trust me. I haven't forgotten. I only have two more days left as well to complete my mission. So let's get our things together and step onto the road that will be our destiny."

As soon as he said that I remembered the dream again where the Dalai llama said, "If you meet the Buddha on the road, kill him."

# Chapter 28

That morning we left, the sky had no color. The fog hovered over the new garden like a ghost.

Grace came out to the cottage. "I brought you some sandwiches for the road. I wish I could take you to Mentone, but I have to be here to attend the funeral. I'm sure you understand." She handed the sandwiches to Pooh and put her arms around him and gave him a kiss on the forehead. "Thank you for all you are and all you did for Billy and well, just thank you so much. You look after this former, recovering redneck for me, will ya?" she pointed to me and smiled. "And you, come with me." We walked outside and stood holding hands. "If you think this is over between us you have another think coming. If you don't come get me, I'll come get you. Now you go do what you got to do with your son and Pooh and whoever, but when you're done, mister, you and I are going to be together. Got it?"

She threw her arms around me, bent me over backwards, and kissed the hell out of me.

"I won't say good-bye because it isn't. You and Pooh hop in the van and I'll take you out to Highway 72. Pooh told me yesterday that 72 is where you will meet your ride to Mentone."

We got in the van. "Pooh, Grace says we are getting a ride out on 72. It would be nice if you would warn me about these things.

Who is picking us up this time, and promise me there will be no detours. I got to get to my son before he leaves."

"Yes, and I still have to get to you before I leave. So let's get going, shall we?"

We said our good-byes to Grace and we stood at the intersection of Woodward Avenue and 72. And there we stood for five hours, or least that is where I stood. Pooh sat down on the grass and did his finger-thumb thing. Teenagers passed and one threw an empty beer can at us just barely missing us. I shot them a bird. A bus full of Japanese tourists drove by and several stuck their heads and cameras out the windows and snapped our picture. I was getting so pissed off the longer we stayed there and the more people passing us by. "Pooh, are you sure this is where we are supposed to be?"

"Trust me. This is the spot. Wherever you are that is where you are supposed to be. Patience."

"You know you've said that a lot to me on this trip. How do you ever really know who to trust? I think for me to learn to trust at this point in my life would be a miracle."

"Speaking of miracles . . ."

"Sweet Lord, help me, I hear another story comin.'"

"This is an old Hebrew tale. Once upon a time there were two brothers, both farmers who raised wheat. One brother had a wife and seven children, while the other was a bachelor who lived alone.

"Every night the bachelor brother would worry about his brother and all the mouths he had to feed, so he would get up in the middle of the night and take sacks of his own grain and pour it into his brother's storage bin.

"Every night the brother with the large family would wake up and think about the fact that he had so many sons who would take care of him in his old age, but his brother had none. So before the sun would rise he would pour sacks of grain into his brother's storage bin.

"Each morning they'd both wake and when they'd look into their respective bins, they'd see they had the same amount of grain as the night before. They wondered if this was a miracle, and it was.

"One night after years of sharing their grain with each other but without the knowledge, they happened upon each other in the middle of the night and understood that miracles are just love in action. It is said that the spot they met and embraced is where the first temple in Jerusalem was built."

That story actually made sense to me. I was becoming downright intellectual. "So if we believe we're all connected and show each other love—"

"That is a miracle and the basis of trust."

"Well, that's a nice thought, Pooh. I don't think any of these drivers on 72 are wantin' to show us any love."

"Trust me."

Oh, brother. I dropped my face into my hands. "I'm just saying, my patience is wearing pretty thin. If one more person comes by and throws something..." I stopped and Pooh jumped right square into my silence.

"Remember your friend the Dalai Llama? He said, 'Enemies and unfriendly people like some of those who have passed up the opportunity to be our friends are some of the most important people to us, because it is only in relation to them that we can develop patience. Only they give us the opportunity to test and practice patience. Not your spiritual master, your friend, or even your relatives, though they do stretch one's patience at times, but it is your enemies and unfriendlies that give you such a great opportunity."

"Great! Let's hear it for Dalai," I said, clapping my hands in his face. "But now I need a ride."

Two more hours went by. By then we had been standing—or in Pooh's case—sitting for nearly seven hours. It was just about getting dark-thirty. "I ain't any closer to my son than we were when we started this morning."

"Oh, that's not true. Trust me. You are closer than you think."

And, yes, I was getting a little ready to kill the Buddha or at least pinch his head off if someone didn't pick us up soon.

Just about that time, an eighteen-wheeler pulled over and I helped Pooh to his feet. I ran to the truck and Pooh walked as slow as any Southerner on a real hot day. I pushed Pooh into the back. I turned to say thank you, and damn if it wasn't a woman trucker and shit fire, she was a big'un! But I didn't care about any of that. I just wanted to get going and go see my son before it was too late.

"Get in here boys and let's get'er'done. I'm Carolyn Mann and don't worry about these," she said, pointing to her chest. "I can drive any man off the road."

I sure did believe her.

"What's ya'lls names? She looked at me and then Pooh in her mirror.

"My name is Billy Bob Coker but you can call me Bubba, and that back there is Pu Tai and you can call him Pooh. Hell you can call him anything, just don't call him late for supper, he loves to eat. Oh, yeah, and he loves to tell you things that are going to happen before they do. He has you know ESP—extra, special, powers—believe it or not."

"Oh, Honey, I believe, I believe, and I believe he's about the cutest thing these old eyes have ever seen," she turned and looked at him and smiled. "Me and him are going to get along real good, aren't we darlin'?"

Pooh giggled and winked at her like a schoolboy.

We pulled out onto the highway and headed north.

"Where you boys headed today?" she said as she started running through her gears.

"We're going to a little place up in the mountains. I'm sure you don't know it. Most people who live in Alabama have never even heard of it. I hadn't until recently and I've lived in north Alabama all my life."

"I doubt I don't know a town in Alabama. I've driven through most of it. What is it?"

"Mentone, up on Lookout Mountain."

"Hell, boy, I'm from Valley Head and that's where I'm headed, dead-heading home for a few days. Valley Head is only five or six miles from Mentone and uphill all the way. So you and cute thing back there hold on. As soon as I get past this place where I know the bears roost, I'll put the pedal to the metal."

Sure enough about two minutes later, two state troopers were in ambush on a little dirt road that came into 72.

Miss Carolyn obviously loved her truck, which was almost brand-new, only having a little over ten thousand miles on it. It was dark blue and so shiny you could part your hair looking in the side of it. It had several horizontal bands, red and powder blue. On its roof, it had two huge antennas, which were painted red, white, and blue. It had a bug screen protecting its nose.

"So how did you become a truck driver? There's not that many women doing this sort of thing," I said.

"There are more and more of us all the time. I worked in two of the big sock factories in Fort Payne making hourly wage, taking orders, and being harassed by the rednecks, no disrespect intended," she looked at me. "I decided I wanted to be my own boss and I was pretty good with tractors and trailers and trucks, having grown up on a farm just outside of Dog Town as a kid."

Like I said, she wasn't petite. She had long brown hair, pulled back into a ponytail and covering it was an Auburn University baseball cap. She sported blue jeans and a plain white T-shirt and wore some pretty-good-looking shit-kicker cowboy boots.

Miss Carolyn kept looking back at Pooh, and Pooh was beginning to eyeball her pretty good as well. I have to say she was pretty good-looking for a big woman.

Finally, Pooh spoke up, "Tell us more about getting started in this line of work."

"Well aren't you the polite one to ask about little ol' me. I got divorced in 1976 from a man who liked his liquor too much and my face not enough, if you know what I mean. I was thirty-five. I traveled around a little after I quit the sock factory and for some reason I took a temporary job as a cook at a truck stop over in Adairsville, Georgia. One day on a smoke break I saw this old boy changing a headlamp on his rig and we got to talking. His name was Tony. I found out he was an independent. And right then and there I asked him if I could come along with him. He said yes, I went in and took off my apron, and we took a load of lettuce to California. Three months later I bought his truck—a 1976 Peterbilt with a skillet face. A few months later I got me a refrigerated trailer. Later I bought a tanker and hauled orange juice and liquid chicken feed and finally I switched to chemical transport. Now I've got this brand-new baby here," she said, padding the steering wheel. She paused and looked back at Pooh. "I'll talk your ear off if you let me. It gets kinda lonesome in here sometimes."

"Is there pretty good money in trucking?" I asked.

"It all depends. Truck drivers make about sixty or seventy thousand a year if they belong to Teamsters, but very few are union. Mostly we're pretty much all non-union and those who don't own their own rigs make about thirty-five thousand. Specialists like auto-haulers can make a hundred thousand a year. An owner-operator like myself can make about the same, but about half of that is overhead—payments on the tractor, road taxes, and about twenty thousand a year on fuel costs." All of a sudden she pulled over to the side of the road.

"What are we doing?" I asked nervously.

"Pooh, darling, why don't you get your sweet buns up here and let little Bubba get back there so you and I get better acquainted? Bubba you get some rest. You look tired and before you know it we'll be in Valley Head, home sweet home."

She was right; I was beat right down to my socks. I climbed in the back and lay down on the bed and looked around. She had a copy of *The Paris Review* (whatever that is), Cormac McCarthy's novel *Border Trilogy*, *The Farmer's Almanac*, Joseph Campbell's *A Hero With A Thousand Faces*, a copy of the *Wall Street Journal*, and a few posters of different jazz festivals from around the country. As I was dropping off to sleep I'd hear her use words like "dilettante" and "circadian rhythms" sprinkled between "shit" and "fuck."

I woke up just as we were coming into Decatur. She geared the truck down, and I heard or at least I thought I heard her say she was a student of Zen Buddhism and that she goes to San Francisco every so often to study at a zendo there and had a master. She asked Pooh if he would like to go there sometime when she took some time off.

"I wish that I could and more than you know, but I only have a little time left before I must return home," he said, which surprised me.

I went back to sleep, thinking Pooh and Carolyn were two peas in a pod. When I woke up again we were going up Sand Mountain, which is just across from Lookout Mountain. I heard Miss

Carolyn saying to Pooh, "If you choose your gear right, and your Jake's on maxi, you can go down a hill without any brakes at all and that saves lots of money over the long haul." She geared down from twelfth to eighth, and said, "I'm not going to use an ounce of brake pressure."

Pooh looked at her and took her right hand in his in between shiftings as we were going down Sand Mountain from Rainsville to Fort Payne. "Perhaps you can teach Bubba back there how to not use his brakes so much with the life he has left."

"We're almost home, little Bubba. Did you have a nice nap?"

"What time is it?" I asked.

"You taking medicine?" she grinned.

"No. I just need to know."

"It's almost midnight. You boys come on home with me and we'll spread some quilts and get a good night's sleep." She winked at Pooh, "And sweet cheeks, you can sleep with me and I'll keep you warm all night long."

"How could any man turn down an invitation like that," Pooh said, grinning from ear to ear.

"Sorry, Miss Carolyn," I said glaring at Pooh. "I got to get to my son in Mentone. He's leaving in the morning for the airport; my ex-wife said he'd be gone by eight in the morning. I got to get to him. So if you would, I'd appreciate it if you carry me on to Mentone tonight."

"Sorry, hon', but I'm about to fall asleep at the wheel. I've been up way past legal limit. Two days I've been burning up this road trying to get home. I can take you in the morning if I get five or six hours of sleep. I'd let you take my pickup but it's in the shop getting the engine overhauled. So you boys come on home with me."

I broke into a sweat and whispered into Pooh's ear. "You've gotta make her take me. I only have a little time left, and I'll need every bit of it to try and make things right with my boy before he takes off. Tell her she's got to do it."

Pooh looked at me real serious like. "Bubba, there once lived a Zen master ..."

"I don't want a story or a lesson, I just want to get to my son before it's too late!"

"A student from the university visited a Zen master. The student asked him, 'Have you ever read the Christian Bible?' The Master said, 'No, read it to me.' The student opened the Bible and read from St. Matthew: 'And why take ye thought for raiment? Consider the lilies of the field, how they grow. They neither toil, neither do they spin, and yet I say unto you that even Solomon in all his glory was not arrayed like one of these. . . . Take therefore no thought for the morrow, for the morrow shall take thought for the things of itself.' The master said, 'Whoever uttered those words I consider an enlightened man.'"

I could tell this was gonna be a long one, so I dropped back on the seat and prayed for death.

"The student continued reading, 'Ask and it shall be given you, seek and ye shall find, knock and it shall be opened unto you. For everyone that asketh receiveth, and he that seeketh findeth, and to him that knocketh, it shall be opened.' The master remarked, 'That is excellent. Whoever said that is not far from Buddhahood.'"

"I finally understand. And after I see my son, I'll think more about it, but right now I'm tired and I just want to get goin.'"

Pooh looked at Miss Carolyn, who was still holding his hand in between shifting.

"So I guess you boys are spending the night. I'll take you little Bubba up the mountain first thing in the morning," she said as her brakes went shhhhhhhh and we came to a stop in her driveway.

I was about to come out of my skin. "Pooh, I've got less than eight hours to find my son, talk to him, and you have to help me. I can't do this by myself. I don't know what to say. You have to come with me. Tell the Wise Ones to send us another ride right here and right now. I'm begging you. I haven't asked you for one thing on this whole trip. You've said 'trust me' a dozen times and I've done so, haven't I?"

Pooh and Miss Carolyn stopped in the driveway and looked at each other with the kind of look that says, "We have to make hay while the sun shines," or in this case the moon shines. She seemed to get it that he wasn't going to be around for very long.

"Goddamnit Pooh, you're the fuckin' Buddha! You ain't supposed to be interested in women or sex and shit. You are supposed to be helping people and right now I'm the people you need to be helping get to his son, not this horny woman!" With each word I kept getting louder and louder.

"In the morning," Pooh said, as he and Miss Carolyn started walking away from me.

Something snapped in me and I pulled out my pocketknife and ran towards Pooh and grabbed him as he was walking away from me. I put my arm around his neck with one arm and held the knife at his throat with the other. "Pooh, I don't want to do this but you are going to tell Miss Carolyn to get back in the truck and drive us to Mentone to see my boy or else. Got it?" As I held the knife to Pooh's throat my eyes were filling up with tears.

# Chapter 29

"Turn him loose," Miss Carolyn said real gently. "You don't want to hurt him. He told me all about your life and all you've lost. If you hurt the only man you have ever loved and who has ever loved you, neither of you will have accomplished your missions. Yes, you may see your son but instead of him seeing you as the asshole he thinks you are he'll see you as a murdering asshole and you two will never be together. Now put the knife down and come on into the house and we'll all forget this ever happened."

"Say something Pooh. Say you'll make her go. Say you're going with me to help me get my son back. Say it Pooh, Goddamnit!"

"Remember your dream? Remember your being told 'Kill the Buddha?'" he whispered as the knife pushed farther against his neck.

"Don't make me hurt you. Screw the dreams," I said about as softly as I could and still be heard.

"No, it is time you listen to your dreams. Listen to the voice inside you telling you what you must do. You must kill the Buddha wherever you find him."

"So you mean I'm supposed to slit your damn throat, and then what? I'll be all enlightened like you? If you're so enlightened, how did you let yourself get in this fix in the first place? And besides, you always know what's going to happen before it does. You could have stopped all of this before it ever started. You could have gotten us a ride all the way to Mentone if you had wanted to."

"Free will. Free will. You have it and I hope you choose to kill the Buddha."

"Don't do anything you will regret little Bubba. Put down the knife and come on inside. We'll find your son in the morning," Miss Carolyn said.

I looked up at the sky and I screamed as loud as I could, "Forgive me!" I let Pooh go and I took the knife and threw it as hard as I could into the woods that surrounded Miss Carolyn's house. "I'm not going in. I'm going to find my son. I'm going without you Pooh, Buddha, whoever the hell you are. I'll walk up the goddamned mountain by myself if I have to. You two can do whatever you need to do. This is what I got to do and I guess I got to do it by myself."

I started walking out of her yard. Pooh came towards me, "I'm going to say this one more time—Trust me—remember your dreams and never forget that you are no less or no greater than any man who has ever lived. You just killed the Buddha and now my mission here is complete. Now you can remember who you wanted to be. Now you can choose how you want to live your life. Now I am free to choose my path. When you finish with your son, come back here and I will tell you what path I have chosen and will hear what you have chosen as well. We will see each other again in the early evening. There is no anger in me towards you, nor will there ever be. Trust me."

He hugged me and kissed me on both cheeks and I walked out to the road and there was not a car or truck anywhere in sight. It was almost as if the world had ended and somebody forgot to tell me.

# Chapter 30

The night was as dark and as desperate as my soul. Valley Head was more like Valley Dead. Not a sound except the wind blowing through the trees. I walked by the First Baptist Church and wondered if my granddaddy was rolling over in his grave, me having been with a Buddhist and gay people for the last seven days. I passed the First Methodist Church and the sign out front said, "YOUR SUFFERING WILL SOON COME TO AN END." On the next block was an old, dilapidated house that had a spirit tree in the front yard. The old, dead tree had blue and green bottles on all its limbs and branches to keep bad luck, haints, and ghosts away from their house. Finally, I got to the main road that led up the mountain and just as I did it started sprinkling rain. I walked by the Dollar General and then past the Woodmen of America Hall. I kept hearing the old country song in my head and started singing it out loud. "You got to walk that lonesome valley, you got to walk it by yourself, no one else can walk it for you, you got to walk it by yourself . . ."

After singing it for a while I heard myself repeating the twenty-third Psalm, "The Lord is my shepherd; I shall not want . . . he leadeth me beside the still waters, he restoreth my soul. . . . Yea, though I walk through the valley of the shadow of death, I will fear no evil . . ."

Then it started raining harder as I walked up the mountain. I walked maybe a half a mile and then it started thundering and lightning. The lightning was a little too close for comfort. About fifteen or twenty minutes up the mountain, it started raining cats and dogs. I was soaking wet. About four in the morning I was half way up and I guesstimated I'd be at the top in Mentone in about two more hours. I was standing on the left side of the road at an overlook where cars could pull in and thank God an SUV with about four fellas pulled over to the side of the road.

The one on the passenger side rolled down his window. "Hey bud, you're gonna get wet out there. What you doing out here all by yourself walking?"

The one doing the talking was a real skinny fellow with a bushy beard that was mostly gray from what I could tell.

"I'm going up this mountain to go visit my son. I sure could use a lift," I yelled and then walked over to his side of the car.

"Well, look at you," came from a voice in the backseat as he stuck his head out his window.

I looked at him and he didn't look none too friendly. "You from around here?" He sounded older; he had a military haircut and tattoos all over his arms.

"Yes, sir, I'm from Scottsboro."

"Who's your people?"

"The Cokers over in Scottsboro and Woodville."

The driver poked his head around the guy in the passenger seat. It was dark, but I saw three teeth holding on for dear life. "Did you say Coker? Is your son Lucius Coker?"

My face lit up. I thought for sure now I'd get a ride. Everybody knows everybody in these parts or we are kin to them. "Yes sir, that's my boy. He lives up here in Mentone," I said as I reached for the door handle.

"You mean up here with the rest of the liberal, nigger-lovin' faggots? I bet you are ashamed to tell anyone you're his daddy!"

"What do you mean?" I was cold, wet, and getting angrier by the minute.

"Didn't you know your son is one of them Civil Liberties faggots who always protests at the State Prison against capital punishment and everyone of them is card-carrying members of the NAACP?"

"Listen here, I just want a ride up this mountain. You fellas going to be good neighbors and give it to me or what? My son and what he does is his business and none of yours or mine."

"Well, if that's true then I guess if you are one of us then you will want to hop in 'cause we're on our way to Menlo down the mountain in Georgia."

"Yeah," said the bushy-bearded guy in the back. "We're heading for a meeting of true Southerners and you can come along and show us you're against the shit your son stands for I reckon. So hop on in brother." The back door flew open.

I stood there for a minute as the water soaked and chilled me. "Thanks, I think I'd rather walk up this mountain," I said as I turned to walk away from souls maybe darker than my own but not by so much that I could judge them, but I sure didn't want to associate myself with anything they stood for or against.

"Oh, so you are like your son, a nigger lover, huh? You think you're too good to ride with the likes of us?" said the older guy in the back.

"Listen, I don't want no trouble with you fellas. So I'll say goodnight to ya and take my leave, if that's all right with you."

The driver poked his head around again. "Well, I don't think it is all right. Maybe you did teach your son not to hate freaks," he said.

I thought to myself that I wish it had of been me, but knew it was his mother, and they must have been reading my mind or maybe I said it out loud because that's when the driver said, "We don't need no more of your kind around here." He looked at the guys in the SUV. "Do we boys?"

About that time everyone but the driver jumped out and the guy in the backseat swung his door hard into me and I fell down. One punched me in the stomach while the other two who were built like football players held me. The driver came around and popped me pretty good in the face a couple of times, and said, "Haul your ass back down this mountain, asshole!"

I stood up, holding my stomach, and spit out a mouthful of blood. "I'm going to see my son!"

"Well, we'll just see about that. Boys." Two of them pushed me backwards as hard as they could and I fell pretty far down into a ditch about thirty or forty feet below and hit my head on a rock or something 'cause I was out cold.

When I finally woke up I was soaked to the bone; leaves and dirt and shit all over me. My face was bleeding and so were my knees and elbows. When I finally cleared my head enough to get up, my right leg collapsed right under me and I fell back to the ground. Then it began raining harder than ever. I swear I saw frogs falling from the sky. It took me a few moments to realize I'd sprung my ankle or something because I couldn't put any weight on it hardly at all.

As I was lying on the ground, I knew I was not going to get up the rest of the mountain and that my son was going to be gone. I was ready to throw in the towel, but I didn't have one.

I must have blacked out again or went to sleep or something because I swear to God, I saw Chigger and Blue standing right in front of me and they were looking at me. "Get'er done," said Chigger and then he disappeared. Then Captain Sam was there and he said, "We're all in the same boat with you son," and then in his place stood Billy and Tom and they were just smiling at me. Grace appeared and stood by them, "Let us help you, we love you," she said, and then they all disappeared, and there stood Pooh, "Okay, I'm going to say it one more time, maybe two, Trust Me. You can do this. Get up and walk and go see your son," and then he disappeared.

I looked to my right and saw a tree limb lying next to me that was about five feet long and three inches around. It had a V at the end and could be used as a crutch. I picked it up and put it under my arm and it was just the right height. I struggled to get up and climbed up the cliff I'd been pushed off of and that took another twenty or thirty minutes because I kept losing my footing and every two steps forward I'd fall back. Finally I was back on the road and I was as tired as I'd ever been in my whole life. I felt like I'd been run over by a Mack truck, but I also felt for the first time in my life like I was connected to something or someone bigger than myself.

As tired, wet, and hurt as I was I started walking. Three-quarters of the way up, the rain subsided and became a steady drizzle. The night was beginning to leave and the light slowly was allowing the bushes and trees to be seen.

Don't ask me how, but I started walking faster and faster and I started thinking about Lucius and what I'd say and what I wouldn't and how I didn't want to fight with him or anyone anymore. I thought about Grace, Pooh, Billy, Captain Sam, ole Jim, Miss Carolyn, and Shirley, and then Lucius again, and they all were running through my head and the faster their images appeared the faster I walked and then just as I got to the top of the mountain standing in the road the sun came up and I threw the crutch high above my head like they do in the movies, except mine came down and hit me right on the head. I shook that off and looked around to get my bearings. I was facing east; on my left was the Mentone Springs Hotel and on the right was the Mentone Bed and Breakfast. I looked up to the sky to the Wise Ones and threw my crutch back up in the air and this time it disappeared right into thin air and I yelled, "Thank You, Thank You, Thank You!" and just as I did I heard a car hauling ass up the mountain behind me. I spun around and there was this red 1956 Ford truck heading right towards me, coming pretty fast, and I froze. I couldn't get off the road. I heard the tires screeching. I thought I better just bend over and under and kiss my ass good-bye. I closed my eyes and yelled as hard as I could, "Lucius, I'm sorry, I love you, son!"

# Chapter 31

I opened my eyes to see if I was dead. The truck's front bumper was lightly touching the front of my soaked jeans. If it had gone one inch closer, I'd have been roadkill.

I flopped myself on the hood and hugged it. I was having a genuine spiritual experience. I looked the driver straight in the eyes and saw him crying. I guess he thought he had almost killed me. I patted myself all over to make sure I wasn't dead after all. The driver rubbed his eyes a couple of times as he stared at me through the windshield; something so familiar about that face . . . After a moment, it hit me. It was Lucius.

"Dad, is that you?" he said as he opened the car door.

I tried to swallow the knot in my throat. "Yes, son. It's me."

"What are you doing here on the mountain, in the middle of the road?"

"I came looking for you."

"But, I don't understand," he said, neither of us aware we were standing in the middle of Highway 117. He stuck out his hand like he was going to shake mine. I taught him to do that by the time he was six years old after he tried hugging me to tell me goodnight. Like the fool I was I had told him then that he was too damn old to go hugging any man.

"Neither do I exactly. But I can tell you this right off: I want more than a handshake." I opened my arms wide and gave him the best hug a man from Alabama can give another man. He didn't hug me back much 'cause I think he was in shock, but I didn't care, I held on like a tick on a hound dog. "What are you doing coming up the mountain this time of the morning? I thought you'd be getting ready to go to the airport." As I brushed the hair off his forehead and kissed him the way Pooh had taught me, he struggled a little.

Lucius looked at me like he'd never seen me before. Finally, he found his voice. "I got a call from Mom last night saying she wanted me to come over and see her because she had something she wanted to tell me before I left for England."

"What did she want to tell you?"

He guided me into his truck. A car was coming our way, but stopped at the caution light—the only one Mentone has.

"Mom told me you had called and that you wanted my phone number because you wanted to see me before I left. She said that something in your voice was more different than anytime since she's known you. And that I should listen to what you had to say, if not for your sake then for mine."

"Was that it?"

"No, she wanted me to know some of the good things about you and she thought she'd better tell me before I left in case we didn't hook up," he said, pulling into the parking lot of Dessie's Country Kitchen. "I got to tell you I wasn't sure I wanted to hear them."

"Well, I'm pretty sure that only took a minute or two," I laughed, poking him in the ribs, trying to swallow back the jumbled feelings I had: relief, joy, and sadness all rolled into one.

"Just the opposite, Dad. We actually talked all night until about an hour ago and I realized it was almost dawn and that I had to get home and finish packing."

I blinked hard. "Well, somebody slap me. I think I'm actually happy."

Lucius looked me over with a concerned frown. "It looks like somebody already did that."

"Would you let me carry you to the airport so we can talk?"

"Are you sure you want to do that?" Lucius said.

"Sure I'm sure."

"Guess you want to ask me the usual stuff—what kind of gas mileage my truck here gets, what the weather is like where I'm going, and how I plan to make a living?"

"I don't want to talk about the superficial stuff we've always talked about and I don't want to fight anymore."

"Me neither, Dad," he said as I put my hand on his while he was shifting gears.

"Let's go to my house. I'll fix you something to eat and get you into some dry clothes. You look like a drowned rat."

"You mean you want to put a roof over my head, food on the table, and clothes on my back?" I said with a chuckle.

Lucius and I started laughing real hard and we talked all the way to his house. I told him how I'd met the Genuine Buddha, who I named Pooh and how he had appeared from a suitcase. Lucius looked at me as if I was nuts until I told him about the strange, magical pictures I'd seen inside.

Lucius teared up and I got nervous. "I know this sounds crazy, son, but it's true."

"I know," he said, his voice barely above a whisper.

I smiled although I had no idea why he'd believe a story like that. I told him about Pooh's mission, about Billy and Tom and about Grace. By the time we pulled into his driveway, I'd told him the whole damned unbelievable journey I'd made in the last six days and that, so far, day seven was absolutely the best.

I finally took a breath and looked at my son's face. It was all soft and open like Pooh's. "How come you believe me? I can hardly believe it myself!"

"Get out of the car," he said, with a Cheshire Cat grin.

And there he was sitting on Lucius' front yard, a huge brass statue of a Buddha with the big belly. It was as if Pooh had posed for the statue himself. I couldn't talk. I just looked at my son and he laughed.

"There's more," he said as he ushered me inside his cottage.

Hanging on his walls was a series of pictures. When I saw them, I swear my heart skipped a beat and I felt like I understood everything. Framed in beautiful wood, he had a picture of the snake in circles, a stained glass with roses in it, a Native American sand painting, and a huge painting of the Buddha—exactly like the ones I'd seen in Pooh's suitcase.

"Where did you get these paintings and pictures?" I asked, pointing to each one.

"Long story," he said, smiling. "But you wouldn't believe me."

He scrambled some eggs, heated up some damn good biscuits, and poured us some coffee. I could see he was in a hurry and running late for his plane, but I didn't want this moment to stop.

We wolfed the food down and while he was grabbing his things I looked around his little country cottage. Lucius was definitely not a chip off the old block and for that I was grateful. As I looked through all the fancy books he had I saw titles on psychology, philosophy, and literature. I yelled out jokingly, "Are you sure your momma didn't get the wrong baby at the hospital? Do you read all these books?"

He threw his large duffle in the truck and put his Martin guitar and his laptop in the cab behind the seat. We talked for the entire hour-drive to the Chattanooga airport. It wasn't like any conversation we'd had before. One thing I'll never forget was him singing "Forever and Ever Amen" by Randy Travis. Then I knew he was my son.

"You ask me how long I'll be faithful, well just listen to how this song ends. I'm gonna love you forever and ever, forever and ever, forever and ever—AaaaaaaaMen."

His voice was great. I could see how talented he was and thought, hell, he could make a living as a musician. Then I remembered that's what he'd told me a hundred times.

"Dad, I bet you don't remember giving me that album for Christmas when I was nine years old."

It took me a while to recall that Christmas, but when I did a tear ran down my face. "At least your old man did something right."

We each talked right from inside our guts and hearts and the other one listened. It was one of the happiest hours of my life.

Fathers are supposed to be the ones that teach their sons, or so I'd been taught. But after I hugged him good-bye, I knew Lucius had more to teach me, but the lessons would have to wait until he returned from his trip.

# Chapter 32

I drove his truck back from the Chattanooga airport to Valley Head doing about forty miles an hour, trying to savor everything that had happened. I knew I had to tell Pooh what had happened, as if he didn't already know and to thank him for everything he'd done for me and Lucius.

When I got to Miss Carolyn's house, they were standing in the front yard hugging and kissing and appeared to be waiting for me. When I drove into the driveway, they were smiling and waving. Miss Carolyn blew a kiss towards me and gave another big one to Pooh and he headed for the truck.

"Let's go, Bubba, you can tell me all about it on our way back to Scottsboro to the Unclaimed Baggage. I have made my decision."

While I was sure he knew what had happened between me and Lucius, I wanted to tell him anyway just for the sheer pleasure of it. But I didn't know what decision he was talking about and he didn't know mine because of the whole Free Will thing.

I told him how Lucius asked me to stay at his house and take care of his place while he was gone, and I told him how I supported him to follow his dreams and give his best shot at music and the woman he was going to be with and that I'd be here waiting for him either way it went. Pooh told me about him and Miss Carolyn, leaving out the details, but that being with her, knowing Grace, Tom, Billy, and me had helped him and taught him so much and that he'd been up there so long that he'd almost forgotten the power of human love.

"So, Bubba," he said. "What are you going to do with your one, wild, precious life?" as we pulled into Unclaimed Baggage's parking lot.

"I'm going to my son's little farm in Mentone and I'm going to meditate on just that for a while, though I may do it with a fishing pole in my hand. I'm going to complete the divorce from my last wife and try to make some amends to her and Shirley. I'm going to go over to my momma's house and ask her to tell me some good things that I don't know about my daddy, and then I guess we'll just see I reckon. What about you, Pooh?"

"The Wise Ones sent me down here to teach you something and me to learn something. And we did just that. They told me if I completed my task that I could choose whether to never come back to earth again or come back and be born again one last time. When I first got down here after all those years up there," he pointed to the sky, "and saw the news, the wars, the racism, the cruelty, the diseases that hadn't been cured, prejudice, the hearts and minds that were still being traumatized, I was certain I would get off the wheel. But then I saw how with a little love, a little help, a little Grace, a big Miss Carolyn, a huge healing between a father and a son, that while it isn't exactly heaven, it isn't hell either, and maybe, just maybe. . . . Anyway, I thought, What the heck, let's go around one more time!"

"That's great! You'll be staying then. You can come with me to Mentone and I'll teach you how to fish and eat grits, and you and Miss Carolyn can get hitched and we'll be one big happy family. I don't mean big as in fat, oh, hell, you know what I mean."

"I know what you mean, Bubba, but I have to say good-bye. I've got to get my suitcase first. I have to come back next time without that particular baggage and see exactly where my karma will take me."

"I don't understand."

"I'm saying I have to go up," he pointed to the sky, "to come back down," then pointed to the ground.

"You mean I'm never going to see you again?" I said, a little choked on my words.

"Oh, you will see me again. Trust me; separation is one of this world's greatest illusions. I'll always be with you and you with me," he said as we went to the back room.

I felt hot tears sliding down my cheeks.

"Bubba, Buddha does not refer to a person who lived in India 2,500 years ago. It is the enlightened mind of any person living right now today. The Buddha taught that we all have Buddha nature—that is our essence, whether we know it or not." He opened the suitcase and bells started ringing. This emerald-green light shined brighter than before, and I hoped it would guide him back to his temporary home. The lights were so bright I had to close my eyes, and the last thing I heard him say was, "Trust Me." And when I opened my eyes, Pooh and his suitcase were gone.

I was sure going to miss that big man. But he said we'd see each other again and I believed him. I trusted him.

I packed a bag, walked into Skeeter's office, and thanked him for the job. I told him I wouldn't be coming back and walked outside, looked up in the sky, got in my son's truck, and drove to his house in Mentone.

164

# Epilogue

Lucius and I wrote each other letters every couple of weeks or so and I started working at DeSoto State Park as a park ranger. Shirley, my first ex, called her sister-in-law's second cousin, Jasper Coker, who was the head ranger, and that's how I got the job. Shirley has come over several times to visit. I saw Ginger at the Home Depot, and she's already married to a good guy over in Ider who runs his own automotive repair shop.

I guess I'd been at Lucius' house about five months when Grace showed up on the doorstep. She looked like she'd swallowed a watermelon. She had a bun in the oven that she said got to baking that last night we were together. She said she was coming in and that she'd found a place for her bees with her daddy's ex-army buddy, Rabbit Jenkins, who lived two farms down. And that we would be raising this baby of ours a lot different than we were raised or she would whup my ass.

About four months later our beautiful baby popped out of the oven. I was there for this one. I passed out, but I was there. I was right smack dab in the middle of the delivery room at the Fort Payne hospital. We lit candles, made them turn out those pesky neon lights, and played some soft music by that old guy, Mozart. They looked at me kinda funny but I didn't give a darn. You should see Little Baby Bubba. He's a little fatty and bald as an eagle. But we don't call him Bubba in public or nothing, just at home. His real name is Sid Hart Coker.

About six months after he was born I looked in his crib and saw him sitting up with his back against the rails. His eyes were closed, and I swear what I saw made tears come to my eyes—both of his tiny sausage-looking thumbs were touching his first fingers, making two little circles—two perfect O's—and as I turned to go get Grace to come see, I swear to Buddha I heard him say, "Trust Me."

# Acknowledgments

I want to thank my wife Susan Lee from the bottom of my heart, who believed in me and this novel and for helping, editing, laughing, contributing, and supporting me throughout the entire process. I couldn't have done it without you.

I also deeply appreciate Todd Bottorff and Rachel Joiner at Turner Publishing for their creative, editorial suggestions, which make me look like a better writer than I am and for believing in this project and publishing it.

Many thanks go to my agent Penny Nelson and the Manus Literary Agency, for support, encouragement, feedback, and energy.

Last but not least, I want to thank my fellow Southerners, Alabamians, rednecks, and Appalachian storytellers who I've learned so much from. I wouldn't live any other place.

To contact Richard "Dixie" Hartwell, go to
www.dixiehartwell.com

# Other Books by John Lee

*The Flying Boy*
*The Flying Boy II*
*Facing the Fire*
*The Anger Solution*
*The Missing Peace*
*Courting a Woman's Soul*
*Growing Yourself Back Up*
*The Secret Place of Thunder*
*Recovery Plain and Simple*
*Doctor I'm Scared*
*Writing from the Body*